SAINT ISAAC
AND THE INDIANS

SAINT ISAAC
AND THE INDIANS

Written by Milton Lomask

Illustrated by Leo Manso

IGNATIUS PRESS   SAN FRANCISCO

Cover illustration by Christopher J. Pelicano

With ecclesiastical approval
Published by Ignatius Press, San Francisco, 1991
All rights reserved
ISBN 0-89870-355-7
Library of Congress catalogue number 90–85767
Printed in the United States of America

For Mrs. Clara R. Lomask

CONTENTS

I

WHAT A ROCK!

THE MORNING MIST LIFTED. The broad river, like a heaving mirror, picked up the first glints of the rising sun.

On the little sailing vessel far out in the harbor, a young French priest strained for a glimpse of the western shore. He was Père (the French word for Father) Isaac Jogues. His young eyes were eager. The movement of his hand, as he suddenly grabbed the arm of the taller man beside him, was swift.

"Charles," he said, "there it is!"

The towering cliff of Quebec had come into view. It rose almost straight up, blocking the horizon like the wall of a castle.

At its foot, on a ragged shelf of land, lay the village. It was not much of a place: a huddle of log cabins, a few sprawling warehouses and a store. But in the summer of 1636, the village of Quebec was the talk of wide-awake people everywhere. It was the capital of New France, gateway to the New World.

"A century ago", Père Isaac told his companion, "a Norman sea captain gave this place its name. He was on a ship here in the harbor, just as we are—only his ship was carrying the first white men to come up the Saint Lawrence River.

"When he saw the cliff there," Isaac went on, "the captain of that little ship was amazed. He cried out in his rough farmer's French, *'Que bec!'* meaning 'what a rock!' "

The happiness inside Père Isaac made his words glow. Early in his school days back in France, a man had told him and his classmates about this country. Ever since, Isaac Jogues had wanted to come to What-a-Rock.

His mother had not liked the idea.

"After you become a priest," she had urged her favorite son, "stay in France. Here you can do important work and perhaps become a bishop."

"A bishop?" Isaac had shrugged. "Let others become bishops. All I want is to become a missionary to the Indians in the New World."

He knew what his mother was thinking. It was

what most of his neighbors in the bustling French city of Orléans thought. Life in civilized France, they reasoned, was comfortable and fun, but life in the lonely forests of North America could only be hard and full of danger.

A long, hollow sound broke the stillness around the ship. It came from the fort of Quebec high above the village. The cannon in the fort boomed once, and then again.

Vessels from home did not put in often at this little Canadian outpost. Every arrival was a ceremony. Already the sagging wharves were alive with people.

As the ship nuzzled the wooden pilings, a squad of soldiers filed down the shore, tapping drums. A pack of dogs barked at their heels. Isaac was too excited to see or hear anything clearly. The scene before him was a blur of people, crowding and shouting, of soldiers, of barking dogs.

The next thing he knew, he and Charles were on the dock. As they pushed through the crowd, a tall, rugged man approached. He was dressed in the same kind of black robe and broad-brimmed hat that Isaac and his friend wore. His arms were stretched wide. His big voice rumbled with pleasure.

"Welcome, gentlemen!" he shouted. "Welcome to the wilderness."

He was Père Paul Le Jeune, Superior of the Jesuit

Mission of New France. The three Frenchmen embraced, all talking at once and excitedly.

"Our homes here are very simple", said Père Paul. "But we will do our best to make you comfortable."

Isaac smiled. He had not come to the New World in search of comfort. He stopped Père Paul, who was about to shoulder the luggage.

"I'll carry it", he said.

"We have a hard walk ahead of us", warned Père Paul. "It is only two miles. But it is all uphill, and our roads here are rough."

Isaac soon saw what Paul had meant. He was breathing hard when they arrived at the plateau far up the hillside. In front of them, a wooden stockade enclosed two small buildings made of rough planks and mortar.

"Our mission house", Père Paul started to explain. Then he said: "But you gentlemen must be starved. After we eat, you can meet the other priests. Then we'll talk. I'm sure we have a thousand things to talk about."

"One minute, please", said Isaac. "Where is the chapel?"

Père Paul smiled. "I might have known you would ask that first." He led them into one of the buildings and opened a door on the far side of the room.

It was the smallest church Isaac had ever seen.

There was room only for the tiny altar and a few benches. Isaac glanced around quickly and then sank to his knees before the tabernacle.

He thanked God that he had been allowed to come this far on his journey. He hoped he would not have to stay long in Quebec. Here, except for a few Algonquin Indians, were only Frenchmen. His wish was to live among the Huron Indians in their tree-dark country a thousand miles to the west.

He had been told that it would be a hard journey. He would have to go with the Hurons themselves, in one of their canoes. It would mean traveling up many rivers, through many lakes. There would be rapids and waterfalls. Then he and the Indians would have to carry their canoes and baggage many miles over rough land.

Bowing his head, Isaac asked a favor. It was a favor he had asked many times on the long voyage across the Atlantic and up the Saint Lawrence River.

"Dear God," he said, "wherever I go next, let me be strong. Make me a man after your own Heart."

2

HERE ANYTHING CAN HAPPEN

A T A ROUGH-HEWN TABLE in the shadowy cabin,
Père Isaac was writing a letter to his mother
in Orléans, France.

The leaves of the oak trees close to the window
hung motionless. The steady scratch of the young
Jesuit's quill pen made the only sound in the late-
afternoon calm.

He wrote that he had arrived at Quebec a few
days before. Now he was eighty miles up the Saint
Lawrence River in a wooded hilltop village. The
French called it Three Rivers. The Indians called
it the "Spot-Exposed-to-All-the-Winds".

"Père Paul and I docked at this little trading post this morning", he wrote his mother. "Père Paul is in charge of all our missions in the New World. His headquarters are in Quebec, but several times each year he pays a visit to the priest at the little mission here."

Isaac saw that his pen had gone dry. He dipped it in ink and wrote on:

"We are waiting for the Huron Indians. They come every summer, six or seven hundred of them. They bring furs and pelts and trade them for cooking utensils and porcelain beads."

Silence. Père Isaac nibbled at his quill, wondering what else he could tell the folks back home. He could picture them in the parlor of their big gabled house overlooking the Loire River. He thought of his mother and father, of his five brothers and three sisters, his cousins and uncles and aunts. What a big family they were! What fun they had always had together!

Isaac had promised himself that he would not be homesick in this strange, new land. But for a few minutes, he could not help himself.

He remembered afternoons on the Loire River. It was one of the swiftest flowing streams in France. Bucking its strong currents, he had learned to swim well. And he remembered footraces on the cobblestones of the Loire embankment. Of all the boys his age in his neighborhood, he had been the fastest.

In the adventurous years ahead, he was to be thank-
ful for these and other skills learned in boyhood
play.

In his quick, restless way, Isaac resumed the letter
to his mother.

"I am going to keep this letter open", he wrote.
"Before the mail boat leaves, I will know whether
or not I may go to the Huron country. When I
first came, Père Paul was reluctant to give permission. Now he says he will leave it up to the Huron
Indians themselves. You can imagine, therefore,
how eagerly I await their coming."

Isaac put down his pen, suddenly aware of noise
outside the cabin. He strode to the door, flinging
it open.

People were running down the path to the beach.
Most of them were French fur traders and trappers
in beaver hats and tasseled deerskin jackets. Here
and there were some of the Algonquin Indians who
were spending the summer at Three Rivers.

All were shouting at the tops of their voices:

"Here they come!"

"Up the river. Look!"

Isaac felt a hand on his shoulder. Père Paul had
come out of the second room of the cabin. He
stood, smiling, at Isaac's elbow. Isaac turned to
him. "This excitement—!" His own voice was excited. "Does it mean that the Huron traders are
at last arriving?"

Père Paul shook his head. "They will come later",

he said. "This is a small flotilla of Algonquin warriors."

"They too are traders?"

"No. They have come to visit their relatives here. They want to show off their captives."

"Captives!"

The two Jesuits were hurrying down the hill, pine needles crunching under their boots. Breathlessly, Isaac repeated his question.

"Captives?" he asked.

"One of their runners brought us the news this morning", said Père Paul. "You know, of course, that the Iroquois are the most warlike Indians in this part of the world. The Algonquins have at long last defeated them in a battle. Now they are bringing their captives down the river."

They had reached the edge of the woods. Beyond lay a pebbly beach and a long wharf.

"You will see strange things this afternoon, Isaac", said Père Paul.

It seemed to Isaac that he had seen nothing but strange things since his arrival in New France. None of them, however, had prepared him for the spectacle before him now. Père Paul had spoken of a *small* flotilla. Isaac counted up to fifty canoes, and still the Indian's shell-like barks came skimming down the Saint Lawrence.

They filled the wide river from shore to shore. Twenty-eight special canoes were leading. From each of these, on a pole, fluttered a scalplock.

"The Algonquins", Père Paul explained, "seized those scalplocks in their battle with the Iroquois."

As he spoke, a shout went up from a group of Algonquin women on the shore. All at once, the women dived into the stream. Splashing and chopping at the water, they swam to the canoes and fought over the scalplocks.

"They have a superstition about enemy scalps", Père Paul told Isaac. "Each squaw wants one for her cabin. She believes it will make her husband stronger in war."

A loose drumming sound arose on the river. The approaching Indian *voyageurs,* as the French called them, had ceased paddling. In unison with the others, each one beat his short, wooden blade against the gunwales of his canoe. The women, meanwhile, had swum back to shore. Those who had been lucky enough to grab scalplocks ran off with them.

The fleet drew in. Isaac could see the Iroquois captives now. There were two of them: a tall, copper-colored brave and his squaw. The man and the woman stood in the prow of the first canoe. Their faces were impassive, showing neither fear nor any other emotion. They held their heads high.

When the Algonquin warriors started to sing, the Iroquois captives sang with them. They shouted out the words as heartily as any of the others.

The canoes floated into the shallows. The Indians

leaped into the flashing waters and waded ashore, bringing their prisoners.

No sooner had the Iroquois brave touched land than something happened that left Père Isaac quivering with shock. With animal-like shouts, the Algonquin women flung themselves upon the captive warrior. They beat him with leather straps and ropes. They pounded him with their fists. They tore at his flesh with their teeth.

In anger, Isaac turned to Père Paul. But Paul was no longer at his side. Isaac saw that the tall Jesuit was striding along the beach toward the screaming women. A sharp fear seized him. Surely Père Paul would know better than to try to stop those women. They would tear him to pieces. Isaac started to run, planning to grab Père Paul and hold him back.

A few paces down the beach, he stopped. He saw that it was too late. Already Père Paul stood in the midst of the women. He was speaking to them. Hands held high above his head, the older Jesuit was talking calmly and earnestly in the squaws' own language. As Isaac watched with amazement, the women quieted. One by one, they drew away from the tortured Iroquois, leaving him free.

Père Paul ceased speaking. Shamefacedly, like children who have been scolded, the Indians moved into the forest and along the paths toward their tents and cabins.

Soon the beach was deserted save for the two Jesuits.

What had Père Paul said to the Algonquin women? How had he persuaded them to stop torturing their captive?

That night, as the two priests sat before a fire in the mission house, Père Paul explained.

"It all goes back to last winter", he told Isaac. "Food was scarce. Several times the priest in charge here shared his small supply with the Indians. This afternoon, I reminded them that another winter is coming. I said if they continued to torture their captive, we French would go on being friendly—but that never again would we take food out of our own mouths to give it to them."

Isaac nodded. Even as Père Paul was speaking, his mind had wandered to another matter—the one closest to his heart. "You say", he said to Père Paul, "that the Huron traders will arrive soon. Tell me honestly: Do you think they will take me to their country when they return?"

"Who knows?" A log in the fireplace rolled forward, spitting sparks. "Who knows?" repeated Père Paul, rising and shoving the log into place with his boot. "The Indians are fickle. One minute they love blackrobes, the next they do not."

"Blackrobes?"

"That is what they call us. To the Indians all

priests are blackrobes." Père Paul returned to the only armchair, a wooden frame loosely covered with moosehide. "Whether or not the Huron Indians take you back with them", he said, "will depend on their mood. We hear they are having a hard journey this summer. They may be in a bad mood when they land here."

"And if they are?"

"I am afraid they will refuse to take you."

Père Isaac's effort to hide his disappointment was not successful. The older Jesuit sensed it and leaned forward.

"Take heart, Isaac", he said. "Remember you are in the New World now. Here anything can happen!"

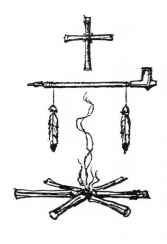

3

INDIAN COUNCIL

THE HURONS HAD ARRIVED! Shortly after dawn, the first canoe was sighted far up the Saint Lawrence. The others followed swiftly, wave on wave.

It was almost noon before all had arrived and the chiefs and braves had gathered on the beach for their dance of greeting. In a line that seemed endless to Père Isaac, the tall and muscular warriors weaved like a giant snake across the pebbly strand. Their chanted song rolled up the green hillsides of Three Rivers.

At dusk, a fire was put to a pile of saplings and pine logs in the yard of the fort. This was the signal for the first council, or meeting. Tonight the Indians would lead the council with the French as guests. Tomorrow night it would be the other way around.

Both nights Père Isaac sat with the other Frenchmen before the council fire. The Indians, many hundreds of them, sat cross-legged on the hard earth or stretched out on the ground. Puffing their pipes, they were still as statues, seldom moving except to rise and speak.

As darkness closed in, the shifting firelight picked out the strange designs on their faces and bodies. One chieftain had a blue nose. He had painted one cheek white and the other black. His neighbor's face was a crisscross of many colored lines.

In the generous use of war paint, the Hurons were like other tribes. What made them look different was their hair. They wore it in high, tufted ridges. Each ridge was about two inches wide, and extended from forehead to neck. Between ridges were wide furrows, made by shaving the head.

The second night's council was opened for the French by a young admiral, the owner of the vessel that had brought Père Isaac to Canada. A brisk, stout man, the admiral wore a crimson doublet and a broad, slouched hat, heavy with ostrich plumes. He spoke in a high voice, almost singing his words. This was the way the Indians spoke. It was the "council pitch".

The night before, the Indians had presented gifts to the French. Now the admiral presented gifts from the French to the Indians.

"Here is a present to grease your arms", he sing-songed, "and to relax them from the labor they have had on the journey. Here is another present to fasten a rope to your canoes to pull them down here next year."

The admiral spoke in French. An Indian repeated his words in the language of the Hurons. When the interpreter had finished, all the Indians grunted:

"Haau! Haau! Haau!"

Père Paul spoke in a low voice, close to Isaac's ear. "That means they approve of what the admiral has said."

"And if they do not?"

"Then they remain silent."

Isaac's heart seemed to stand still. Before long, the admiral would ask the Hurons to take him to their country. Would they then grunt *"Haau! Haau! Haau!"*? Or would they remain silent?

The admiral was talking to the Indians about the children. Three Indian lads had made the long trip from the Huron country. During the coming winter, they would stay in Three Rivers and attend the school recently opened by the Jesuits.

"Now," the admiral was saying to his Indian audience, "we would like you to look at three of *our* boys." He whipped the richly plumed hat from his head and waved it at three French lads sitting not far from Isaac. The boys scrambled to their feet. At a nod from the speaker, they stepped forward so that the Indians could have a closer look at them.

In the flickering firelight, their small forms threw long shadows. Père Isaac could just make out the features of the nearest boy. "The lad with the freckles and the solemn face", he whispered to Père Paul. "Haven't I seen him around the Mission House here?"

"Yes. He lives there. His name is Amyot. Jean Amyot."

"Has he no parents?"

"They died on the high seas", Père Paul shook his head sadly. "It was a great tragedy for the boy. An old gunsmith brought him here."

"Isn't he very young to be going among Indians?"

"He says he wishes to go", Père Paul smiled. "As a matter of fact, I think he's as eager to go as you are."

At a word from the admiral, the boys returned to their places near the fire. The admiral adjusted the brightly colored sash about his waist. Resting a hand on his sword hilt, he once more addressed the Indians.

"We ask you", he said, "to take these boys to your villages for a year or more. If you do not have room in your canoes for all of them, take one or two. Living among you, our boys will learn your ways and come back someday to tell us about them. Meanwhile, your boys will be learning our ways and will return to tell you about them. In this manner, we will gain an understanding of one another. We will become better friends."

Again the Indian interpreter repeated his words in the Huron language. This time, some of the Indians grunted *Haau! Haau! Haau!* Others were silent.

"That means they are undecided", Père Paul whispered to Isaac. "They will debate among themselves and give us their answer later."

Isaac bent forward, tense. The admiral had spoken his name—or rather the name that the Huron Indians had given him. Unable to form the words "Isaac Jogues" in their language, they had already taken to calling him "Ondessonk". It was a Huron word, meaning "bird-of-prey". The Indians had chosen it because of Père Isaac's piercing eyes and quick movements.

"You have brought one blackrobe back to us", Isaac heard the admiral saying. "You have treated him well. We are glad of this. Now we ask you to take with you another blackrobe. I am speaking of the priest you call Ondessonk."

The admiral paused, clearing his throat. "Ondessonk", he told the Indians, "asks nothing from you. He is not interested in buying or selling. He has given up home and family to live among you.

Why? Because he wants to teach you about our God. Will you take Ondessonk to your villages?"

The Indian interpreter repeated the Frenchman's words. When he had finished, not an Indian spoke.

Isaac cast a look of despair at his Superior. Père Paul smiled. Rising, he whispered something in the admiral's ear.

The admiral lifted his hand to signal that he wished to speak further. "We French", he said, "have tried to be good friends to your nation. We have fed you when you were hungry. We have warmed you when you were cold. If you refuse to take Ondessonk with you, we must ask ourselves: Is it possible that the Huron no longer desires the Frenchman's love?"

As soon as these words were interpreted, a brawny chieftain arose. He wore a high bonnet of colored feathers. Large silver bracelets dangled from his nose and earlobes. His flowing fur robe was embroidered on the inside with the dyed quills of the Canadian hedgehog.

In the high council pitch, he spoke on and on. It seemed to Isaac that he would never finish.

When he sat down, another Indian arose. He too spoke at length. After him, another spoke; and then another. The Indians, Isaac noted, spoke without moving their lips. They dragged their words up from the depth of their chests. On and on they spoke, in singing, drawn-out grunts.

Père Isaac's hand went to the big wooden beads of his Rosary. The gesture itself was a prayer. Another prayer formed in his mind. "O Holy Mother of God," he prayed, "you who have helped me a thousand times, help me now."

At last, it came! In chorus, the Indians shouted: *"Haau! Haau! Haau!"*

Père Paul slapped Isaac on the back. "Get ready, my good friend", he cried. "You will be leaving us in a few days."

Père Isaac could hardly believe it! For years, he had dreamed of this moment.

As soon as the council broke up, he rushed to his cabin. From his luggage, he took the letter he had started a few days before to his mother. He had left it open, so he could tell her the Indians' decision. Hastily, he scrawled a line at the bottom of the page:

> P.S. I have just received, within this very hour, the order to prepare myself to depart in three or four days to go among the Hurons.
> *From Three Rivers, 20 August 1636,* Isaac Jogues

He sealed the letter. In the morning, he would hand it to the admiral. It would go to France on one of the admiral's ships.

He left the cabin. Outside the night was warm. A soft moon lighted the path. He could hear the rustle of small animals in the forest. A bird fretted among the oak leaves.

He strode up the hill to where in a grove of wind-twisted fir trees stood the mission chapel. Inside, he prostrated himself before the Blessed Sacrament, words of gratitude on his lips.

He offered his thanks to Our Lady. Over and over he addressed her:

"Oh, Mother of Christ . . . Help of Christians . . . Seat of Wisdom . . . always I have put myself in your hands. And now, because of your prayers, mine have been answered. Because of your help, my deepest hope has been realized. I have been chosen from among a thousand Jesuits far better than myself to carry to the savages of the New World the life-giving sacraments of your divine Son."

An hour passed, and another. The thin light of dawn glazed the windows of the little church. Isaac recalled things Père Paul had told him—the dangers that awaited him in the Huron country; the fact that the Indians might murder him. His eyes lifted to the figure of Christ Crucified; and there came to him, like a voice at his ear, the words of a great French saint:

"Not without reason does he ask our life, who has given up his own for us."

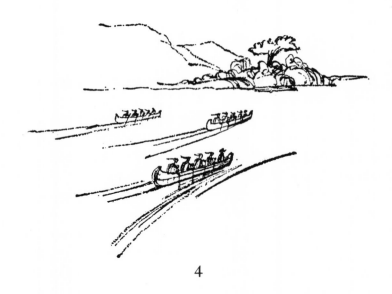

4

A THOUSAND MILES
BY BARK AND PORTAGE

Two INDIANS, knee-deep in the blue-green waters of the Saint Lawrence, held the fragile
canoe firm. Standing on the rock-strewn shore,
Père Isaac tucked his cassock into the sash around
his waist. Then, carefully following the instructions
given him by Père Paul, he removed his boots,
dusted the sand from his feet and carefully, very
carefully, stepped into the gently rocking bark.

His breviary hung at his neck, held by a leather
strap. In his pack was an altar stone. With this,
he could say Mass anywhere. A tree stump could

be his altar, or the rocks on the rim of a lonely cove.

Around him, the other canoes were filling. In one of them sat Jean Amyot. Ten years old, going on eleven, Jean's freckled, solemn face barely cleared the gunwales. The Hurons had taken council among themselves. They had agreed to carry this one French boy with them.

Jean nodded at Père Isaac, and the young Jesuit waved. From the pebbly strand of Three Rivers came Père Paul's booming voice. "Don't even wave, Isaac. Sometimes the slightest movement will turn the canoe over."

Isaac rebuked himself for his carelessness. Made of birch bark, the graceful Indian "ship" was safe so long as everyone sat as still as possible. A careless movement might upset it. A heavy step could put a hole in the thin bottom.

At a signal from a chieftain, the Indians dipped their paddles. Isaac felt the canoe quiver as the Huron flotilla glided into the sparkling waters of the Saint Lawrence. Back on the slowly vanishing beach of Three Rivers, Père Paul made the sign of the cross in the air, blessing the fleet.

Père Isaac was on his way to the Huron country, a thousand miles to the west.

The Huron paddlers rocked back and forth. Their precision amazed Isaac. Every second, every blade dipped exactly eighteen inches into the shimmering depths, rose, was pulled forward and dipped again.

Each Indian voyageur sat on his heels. His shins lay against the frame of the canoe, so that his knees rose almost as high as his chin. Père Isaac sat in the same position. He had never sat in one position so long before. At first it was merely uncomfortable. Soon, it became painful. His back and his legs ached.

They had started in the cool of the morning. As the sun wheeled higher, the treeless highway of water became unbearable. The sun penetrated the nightcap Isaac had been told to wear, instead of his hat, so as not to obstruct the view of the voyageurs. Perspiration beaded his forehead and rolled into his eyes. He blinked repeatedly, fearful of lifting a hand lest he unbalance the canoe.

At midmorning, the fleet rode out of the narrows into a wide expanse of the river called Lake Saint Peter. The canoes moved close to the northern shore, alongside waving grass. They glided past bays and inlets, yellow sand and black swamps. A dozen miles away, the other shore was a shapeless blot.

In the late afternoon, the river narrowed again. The canoes maneuvered among the marshy islands at the head of the lake.

Just as Isaac was beginning to feel that he could

not sit still another second, the fleet nosed into the grassy mouth of a little river. Silently the Indians disembarked.

Père Isaac pulled himself up gingerly, wondering if he could leave the canoe without spilling it. He noticed that the Indians leaped out quickly. Awkwardly, he imitated their movements and sighed with relief when he found both feet firmly planted on the river bottom and the canoe still upright behind him.

He waded ashore. The scene there was one of wordless bustle. He remembered one of Père Paul's last-minute instructions. "Whenever you make camp," the Jesuit Superior had advised him, "pitch in and help the savages. They do not admire an idle person. Find work to do."

But what work? He looked around. A hundred paces away, he saw an Indian carrying a heavy bundle, one end of which dragged on the ground. He hurried toward the man, but before he could reach him, another Indian had come to his aid. He halted, again looking around him, feeling painfully useless and ill at ease.

"Mon Père!"

Turning, Père found the orphan lad, Jean Amyot, at his side. The French lad's small, freckled face was solemn.

"I see you would like to help the Indians", he

said. "They can always use a little green wood to put on the fire at night. If you would like to come with me, *mon Père*, I have an axe."

"Thank you, Jean", said Isaac, grateful for the boy's thoughtfulness.

The lad hurried ahead, stopping at a grove of half-grown trees. Isaac admired the speed with which he felled a few and chopped them into logs. As they returned to camp, each with a load of green wood, Père Isaac studied the lad's face. It was drawn and grave, like that of an old man. "Does this boy never smile?" he wondered to himself.

At the camp site, a mammoth kettle, resting on stones, was already bubbling over the fire. It contained corn, ground between rocks and mixed with water to form a mush. It was unseasoned and tasteless. But Père Isaac was famished and ate eagerly.

"I believe this is the best meal I ever had", he said to Jean. "What do you think?"

The boy nodded. He was not eating much, Isaac noticed; and at intervals he looked around at the Indian faces, his dark eyes big and troubled.

Père Isaac tried to think of ways of coaxing him to talk. "Père Paul tells me", he said, "that an old gunsmith brought you to Three Rivers."

Again, the boy merely nodded. Perhaps, thought Isaac, he's uncomfortable around priests. Or perhaps . . . ! He studied the freckled, solemn face more closely. Yes, that was it! The boy was frightened. For all his manly air, he was frightened.

"Tell me, Jean," he said gently, "have you a patron saint?"

"A patron saint?" The boy spoke slowly. "Should I have one?"

"We have a long, hard journey ahead of us. We are headed for a strange, wild land. Personally, I am frightened."

The boy looked up. There was amazement in his dark eyes—and something else: relief, perhaps, at discovering that even the priest was frightened of what lay ahead. *"You?"* he said to Isaac. "You, *mon Père*, are frightened?"

"Naturally, Jean. I've asked Our Blessed Mother to protect me. She's my patroness. Now, whom shall we select for you?" Isaac recalled what Père Paul had told him—how Jean had lost his parents on the ocean voyage from France. "Your parents are dead, are they not, Jean?"

"Yes, *mon Père*. There was a lot of sickness on the ship. First Mama died and then . . ." The thin voice broke. "Then—then Papa!"

"And you miss them very much?"

The boy nodded vigorously.

"Well then," said Père Isaac, "I know just the saint for you." He reached into his pack, lying

beside him, and brought out a handful of the medals
he had brought along for the Indians. He chose
one and placed it in the boy's hand.

For some moments, Jean looked at it in silence.
Isaac could see that he was fighting tears. He looked
away, so as not to embarrass him.

After a while, the boy found his voice. "It's Saint
Joseph", he said.

"Yes, Jean. The foster-father of Our Lord. He
can be your foster-father too, if you wish. Whatever
you need, ask him for it. He'll always help you."

The boy looked at the medal in his hand. "Thank
you, *mon Père*", he murmured. He got to his feet.
"If you'll excuse me—I have a chain in my pack.
I'll put the medal on it."

Isaac nodded. He watched as the boy hurried
across the clearing to the rock under which he had
hidden his belongings.

Darkness came fast. Soon all members of the
voyaging party were stretched out either on the soft
turf near the river or farther inland on the grass
of a shallow incline.

Père Isaac could not sleep. He was acutely aware
of the forest nearby. Mosquitoes buzzed at his head.
Other insects shrilled in the underbrush. From the
near distance came the occasional wail of a wolf
or the scream of a nightbird.

Suddenly Père Isaac sat bolt upright. After Jean
had gone to find his chain, Isaac had lost track of

him. Now a terrible thought entered the priest's mind. Suppose, during the night, one of the Indian braves took it into his head to kill the boy!

He knew that some of the Indians resented Jean. They felt that the space he took up in the canoe could have been better filled with tools and trinkets.

Picking up his blanket, Père Isaac went searching for the child. Some forty paces distant, he found him. Jean lay in a hollow formed by the roots of an oak tree.

Curled up like a fist under his blanket, the boy was sleeping soundly.

Père Isaac sighed with relief. He raised a hand in blessing and then found a place for himself nearby. Now his mind was at ease. He breathed one last prayer, and lay down to sleep.

Toward the end of the first week, the Huron fleet left the Saint Lawrence. It headed north and west up a swift and ragged stream that reminded Isaac of the Loire River in front of his Orléans home.

They had not gone far when he heard a distant boom-boom like drum beats in a hollow space. As they proceeded, it grew louder—and still louder. Soon it filled the gorge with a moving wall of sound that closed them in and seemed to narrow the world to this single, raging slice of water. They pushed around a rocky point of land. Before them lay the source of the sound—an oncoming rush of white-capped water. Their eyes searched the distance, but the stream seemed to be filled with jagged rocks. This meant that they could no longer proceed by water.

The Indians poled their canoes into a backwash and jumped out. Shouldering their luggage and toting the canoes on their heads, they scrambled along the stony shore for miles. This part of the journey was called a portage.

This was their first portage. There were to be many more.

A few days later, as they crept along a slippery clay bank, Jean Amyot fell. Isaac hurried to the boy's side.

"Shall I carry you, Jean?"

"No, thank you, Père Isaac. I am all right."

The boy walked on bravely, but Isaac could see that he was limping. That night after they had eaten and bedded down, Isaac went to where the boy was lying. Jean was shivering in his sleep. The Jesuit touched the lad's forehead. It was hot with fever.

At their first portage the next day, Isaac hoisted the lad to his shoulder. The path lay along a rocky bank above a waterfall. Several times, Père Isaac slipped. Once he almost fell.

He wished he could walk as well as the Indians. Wearing light shoes or even barefoot, they padded along as if the rough land were a cabin floor.

Père Isaac was terrified at the thought of falling

and hurting the boy. "If only I could persuade one of the Indians to carry him", he thought. He tapped the shoulder of a husky brave. With many gestures, he asked him to take Jean in his arms. The Indian grunted and shook his head. He spat on the earth alongside the path and pointed to it.

"He doesn't understand you, Père Isaac", said Jean.

"He understands, all right."

The Indian, Isaac knew, was telling him to leave the sick boy there. That was the law of the trail. Among the Indians, it was every man for himself. If one were wounded or became ill on a journey, he was left where he fell. The others went on, leaving him to die.

Père Isaac thought hard. Somehow, he must persuade one of the Indians to carry Jean.

Suddenly a plan suggested itself.

He noticed that one of the Hurons always carried the big war hatchets. When the caravan halted for a brief rest, he approached this man.

The brave had squatted on the earth. The hatchets lay beside him. Putting Jean down, Père Isaac scooped up the hatchets. As he lifted them, he grunted and groaned. Then, putting the hatchets down, he picked up Jean, smiling broadly as he did so.

The Indian got the idea. Jean, he saw, was much lighter than the hatchets.

After that, Père Isaac carried the war hatchets

on all the portages. They were a heavy and awkward burden. Once, staggering along a narrow ledge, he lost his balance and all but tumbled into the roaring waters below.

But Père Isaac knew that if he fell with the war hatchets, he would hurt no one but himself. Meanwhile, on the shoulders of the sure-footed Indian, little Jean was safe.

By the nineteenth day, they were again traveling by water. Throughout the long journey, the Indians had been glum. Even among themselves, they had exchanged few words. But now all this changed. A shout of joy went up from every throat as the fleet swept out of a little river into the largest inland body of water Père Isaac had ever seen. It was Lake Huron, as the French had named it. The Indians called it the Fresh Sea.

Now the voyageurs dug and pulled their oars as never before. The canoes skittered over the bright waters. Suddenly the tree-shaded arms of a cove surrounded them. Above the little bay, along the crest of a hill, loomed an Indian village.

The villagers themselves thronged the sandy beach: squaws and children, young braves and ancient ones, gnarled as the trees they stood under. As the first canoes swept into view, the beach came to life. The braves and ancients flung themselves into a ceremonial dance. The women and children clapped and shouted. In the canoes, the homecoming voyageurs chanted.

Down the path from the village hurried five men in the black robes of Isaac's Order.

At the sight of them, Isaac forgot all his lessons in canoeing. Grasping the gunwales, he pulled himself to his feet.

In this manner, recklessly waving his nightcap, Père Isaac Jogues arrived in the country of the Hurons.

5

AROUND THE HURON FIRES

THE HURON COUNTRY was a wild and rolling one, Père Isaac would soon discover: a country crossed by many streams, broken by many lakes, and darkened by a thousand towering trees.

When he landed that morning in the fall of 1636, he immediately looked around for Jean Amyot. The boy's health had improved during the last days of the journey, but he was still weak. The minute the lad touched shore, Père Isaac hoisted him to his shoulders.

"Hold on, Jean", he cried, pushing through the Indian throng and hurrying up the hill toward the approaching Jesuits. One of them, he saw, had out-distanced the others and was almost to him.

He recognized him at once. It was the famous Père Jean de Brébeuf, Superior of the Huron Mission—the very priest from whose lips, years before in France, Isaac had first heard about the Jesuit missions to New France.

Père Jean was a bluff but gentle giant of a man. People often said that had he not chosen to become a priest, he would have made a great soldier. He had a commanding way about him. He was taller than any Indian in the Huron country, broader of shoulder and stronger. Half in admiration, half in awe, the Indians had named him *Echon*. It was their word for "chief".

"Welcome, welcome!" he shouted as Isaac reached him. "And who is this?" he added, grabbing Jean from the other's shoulder and shifting him to his own.

"Your namesake", Père Isaac told him. "Jean Amyot. He has come to live among the Hurons. He wants to learn."

"Good, good!" cried the tall Jesuit. "And what is it, little namesake, that you expect to learn here?"

"I am going to learn the Huron language", said Jean promptly. During the trip, the child had become more talkative. He even smiled at times. He was smiling now, and staring with some fascination at Père Jean's bushy mustache. "When I grow up," he went on, "I'll be an interpreter."

"With whose help?" demanded Père Isaac.

"With God's help", said the boy quickly. "And Saint Joseph's."

The other Jesuits had joined them. There were introductions. Laughing and talking together, they mounted the hill. A triple wall of strong poles surrounded the village—"the palisades", Père Jean called it.

Inside the palisades, the Indian cabins, or longhouses, were strewn about in no particular order. The hard-packed streets were rough and winding. On the outside, the Mission House looked like the others. Inside it was quite different. The Indians used no partitions in their houses. But the four French workmen who lived with the priests were carpenters; they had built partitions. Instead of deerskin flaps over the openings, as in the Indian houses, they had made strong wooden doors.

There was a big living room, and beyond that, a chapel—one of the loveliest, Père Isaac thought, he had ever seen. They knelt before the rude but handsome altar, the six priests and the boy, and prayed. Père Isaac was almost frightened at the joy in his heart. He prayed for the humility, the courage and the patience that the job ahead would demand of him.

Back in the Mission House living room, he and Jean found themselves the center of a staring crowd that momentarily grew larger and noisier as more and more Indians pushed into the house to have a look at the newcomers. Père Isaac noticed a number of boys and girls. Their piercing black eyes glistened as they peered at Jean from around their mothers' skirts. Suddenly one thin, olive-skinned lad darted into the center. He touched Jean's cheek with his hand and then scurried back to his mother, butting his head against her body and roaring with laughter.

Père Jean crouched, speaking to Jean. "These children", he explained, "have never seen a French boy before. You'll like them. That lad you just saw can teach you a lot about hunting. He makes the finest traps of anyone in the village."

"I'll be very glad to learn from him", said little Jean, smiling. Père Isaac smiled too. It was good to see this boy, once so solemn and silent, now so happy and ready to talk.

All that fall there was much sickness in the Huron country. Père Isaac found himself very busy, heating broth in the Mission House and carrying it to the Indian cabins. Often he sat for hours comforting some mother whose child had died.

Quickly, he mastered the Hurons' jerky language. Daily, he studied their ways.

Like the other North American tribes, the Hurons

were incredibly cruel to enemies. Out on the trail, they observed the Indian rule of every man for himself. But in their own villages, they could be the soul of kindness.

At dawn one morning, a fire swept away a small cabin occupied by a family of orphaned children. Jean Amyot, on his way to visit some traps he had set in the woods, was the first to see the flames. He ran to the Mission House, rousing the priests. They, in turn, hurried from cabin to cabin, calling the villagers.

Everybody pitched in: braves, squaws, children. The priests and workmen from the Mission House did their share.

By midmorning, the Indians had set up two parallel rows of tall, strong saplings. They bent the tops of these till they almost met. Then they lashed them together with leather straps, leaving an opening one foot wide along the top of the house. Split poles were laid across the uprights and attached to them with cords of linden bark.

Meanwhile, large flaps of bark had been stripped from the white cedar trees and the elms. Tendrils were used to fasten these to the frame of the cabin. By nightfall, the children were snug in a new house, generously stocked by their neighbors with food and firewood, cooking utensils and skins.

The first time Isaac entered a Huron home, he had to hold his breath. The Indians knew nothing

of cleanliness. An old utensil, a worn-out garment—
a worn-out anything—was left lying wherever it
had last been dropped. Food rotted in the grimy
dust of the floor. Fleas gathered in damp corners.
The inside of the cabin was a dim tunnel, some
35 feet wide and anywhere from 50 to 240 feet
long. A row of fires, smoldering down the center,
cast fitful shadows on the sooted walls, and on
the rude uprights and beams. These were thickly
hung with weapons, skins and with row on golden
row of unshelled corn.

There were no windows. The smoke escaped
through the opening in the roof. On damp and
cloudy days, it hung in the cabin, a thick and acrid
haze.

Two families lived by each fire. Since there were
no partitions, anywhere from five to twenty families
and as many dogs lived and ate and slept together
in what seemed to Isaac like everlasting din and
disorder.

The Indians trooped in and out of each other's
houses at will. The idea of knocking on a door
struck them as silly and discourteous. The rules
of hospitality were rarely violated. Whoever entered
a cabin—friend or foe, Indian or paleskin—was
given a place by the fire. He had only to dip his
bark or earthen bowl in one of the family kettles
and eat his fill.

Unlike many tribes, the Hurons were farmers.

In clearings beyond the palisades, they grew pump-
kins and squash, beans, corn, hemp and sunflower
seeds.

All autumn the squaws worked in the clearings.
Their hoes were made of wood with stone blades.
A few had iron hoes, purchased from the French
at Three Rivers.

The men did no farming. The women had even
made the clearings. They had done so, Isaac learned,
not by chopping down the trees, but by burning
a section of the forest, tree by tree. A few branches
of each tree were hacked off and placed, with brush-
wood, around the trunk. Then branches and brush
were set afire. Consequently, the field in which
the women worked was black with charred tree
stumps.

Often, walking beyond the palisades, Père Isaac
stopped to talk with the busy squaws.

"I noticed", he told one, "that you use no fertilizer."

"Fertilizer?" The woman rolled the word out
uncertainly, a look of bewilderment in her black
eyes. "What is fertilizer?"

"In my country", explained Isaac, "we put manure on the soil. In other words, we feed it."

The look of bewilderment in the woman's eyes
gave way to amusement. Hurrying to one of the
squaws, she spoke in a low voice, evidently repeat-
ing what Père Isaac had told her.

The other woman laughed loudly. At that, several others came running, clamoring to hear what the blackrobe had said.

"Have I said something funny?" asked Isaac, approaching the women.

"You say you feed your land", exclaimed the squaw to whom he had first spoken. "That is funny. We prefer to let the land feed us."

"But if you put no manure in the soil", protested Isaac, "it will wear out and produce no more food for you."

"Let it!" laughed the woman. "Our village is now ten years old. In another year or two the land will be worn out. We know that, but we don't care. When the time comes, we'll move elsewhere."

"All of you?"

"Yes, all of us. The whole village. Why not? There is always plenty more land."

Back in the village, Père Isaac stopped to chat with some of the old men. At this season, most of the young men were on the trail, hunting or fishing or battling with their traditional enemies, the Iroquois Indians. The old men, left behind, built houses or made weapons or mixed the oil of the sunflower seed with soot or berries or white clay to make warpaint.

Père Isaac watched a bent-backed ancient build a canoe. The Indian ship was a marvel. A baby could put his fist through the side of it; yet a thirty-five-foot bark could easily carry thirteen men and a ton of goods.

First, the old Indian built a frame of thin, seasoned white cedar boards. He covered them with strips of birch bark, sewed together and lashed to the frame with *wattape*, the supple root of the red spruce. He water-tightened the seams with melted pine tree gum.

While the Indians worked, they talked. Back in Three Rivers and on the long voyage west, the Hurons had talked little. Here, it seemed to Isaac, they never stopped.

In spite of the sickness, their cabins rang with laughter. The children played noisily in the crooked streets. Watching them, as he made his rounds of the sick, Père Isaac smiled. Children, he thought, were the same the world around. How many times in his own boyhood had his mother called him "my little Indian". He waved at a gang of boys, clambering about the thatched roof of a longhouse.

Farther down the street, another group of boys were playing a game they called Points. Jean Amyot was among them, for the Indian lads had taken to Jean and he to them.

"Look, Père Isaac", he cried, seeing the priest approach. "It's like a game we play in France."

He came, laughing, to the Jesuit to show him. "Back home", he explained, "we take a little bat with a hole scooped out of the end of it. We throw a musket ball in the air with the bat, and then try to catch it with the bat and throw it again. See— this is just the same." He placed some pine needles on the pointed end of a stick, tossed them into the air—and caught a lot of them, tossing again. At each toss, the Indian boys hooted and shouted, trying to make Jean miss. Soon he did, and the pointed stick was passed to another boy.

Père Isaac walked on. Near one of the palisade's gates, on the lower limbs of an elm, some girls had constructed a house of their own. Their thin voices filtered through the leaves, as though a breed of talking birds had taken roost.

When the first snows came, the hunter braves and the warriors came home from the summer trails. Now the din grew greater and more constant; for in all twenty of the Huron villages, this was the season of festivity. There were deer feasts and bear feasts. There were wild dances, done to the roll of tom-toms and the click of tortoise-shell rattles.

Talk and laughter, song and dance—every day; not until darkness, and often not even then, did silence fall on the lakeside village of Ihonatiria, called by the Indians "The-Little-Hamlet-above-the-Loaded-Canoes".

Among the Hurons was an important chief, noted throughout the tribe as a great warrior and fisher-

man. Although he lived miles away, he often came
to the Mission House to listen to Père Jean instruct-
ing the Indians.

"Name for me", he said to Père Jean one afternoon, "all the rules a man must follow in order
to be baptized and become a Christian."

Père Jean named the rules. "No divorce," were
his last words to the chief, "no superstitions, no
lying, no cheating."

The chief shook his head sadly. The Indians believed in divorce. They were full of superstitions.
They did not look on lying and cheating as serious
offenses.

"Your rules are hard", said the chief, "and very
uncomfortable." And he went away, still sadly
shaking his head.

The Jesuits saw no more of him for several weeks.
Then, one evening, as they were preparing to retire,
he suddenly appeared in the Mission House doorway. He apologized for coming at a late hour, but
said he had something on his mind.

Ordinarily the great chief was a bold man, tall
and strong featured. At this moment, he was shy
as a boy. He lowered his eyes and twisted his long
hands together.

"I have thought about this hard and long", he
said. "I would like to be told more about your
Faith. When you think I know enough, baptize
me. If you consent to this, I promise to be faithful.

I will keep the same squaw all my days. I will throw away my superstitions. I will give up lying and cheating."

The tall chieftain spoke solemnly. Père Jean replied in the same way. "We will start your instructions at once", he said.

In time, the day came. In the tiny chapel Père Jean poured the healing waters and baptized the chief with the Christian name of Peter. Then Père Isaac prepared to offer the Holy Sacrifice of the Mass.

Word of the Indian leader's conversion had spread throughout the Huron country. As the hour for Mass approached, more and more Indians crowded into the tiny chapel. Père Jean said he had never seen so many of them there before.

Putting on his vestments in the living room, which also served as sacristy, Père Isaac said a special prayer to Our Lady. "Holy Mother of God," he prayed, "extend your motherly love and protection to our brother Peter. May he have the grace to be a loyal follower of your divine Son and a living example of God's grace to his fellow Indians."

Then Père Isaac, preceded by Jean Amyot and a French workman, who were to serve his Mass, entered the chapel.

Many of the watching Indians had never seen a Mass before. At first, they were restless and talkative. But as the Sanctus approached, they became

more attentive. The Consecration chimes rang out
in a deep silence. And then, with fascinated eyes,
the Indians watched while their newly baptized
chieftain received his First Holy Communion.

It was a great day for the Jesuits. They had made
many converts in the country of the Hurons, but
so far all had been old people about to die or sick
babies whom they had baptized, with their parents'
consent, just before death. Peter was the first adult
Indian to come to them in full health. Moreover,
he was a person of power and influence throughout
the tribe.

6

CAPTAIN CLOCK

THE JESUITS ROSE AT FOUR O'CLOCK in the morning. After community Mass, they breakfasted. Then the Mission House doors were thrown open, and the Indians pushed in. All day, the braves came and went, or sat around the living room fires, smoking their pipes.

Père Jean and the other priests talked to them about God. They described God's laws. They told the Indians that those who lived by God's laws in this world would live with God himself in the next.

Père Isaac, sitting in on one of these instruction sessions for the first time, paid close attention. "If

I am to help bring Christ to these people," he told himself, "I must first find out how their minds work."

Much that he heard that first afternoon filled him with amazement. "You tell us", a young and brightly painted brave said to Père Jean, "that the same Spirit created us all."

Père Jean nodded. "God made everyone in this room. He is the Father of us all."

The young brave snorted. "Impossible", he said.

"Why do you say that?"

"I say it because of what my eyes see. My eyes see that you French can make knives out of steel and hoes out of iron. My people cannot do so. If we were both created by the same Spirit, he would have taught us Indians how to make those things too."

Patiently, Père Jean replied to this strange argument. "God", he said, "does not teach us to do these things. He simply gives each of us the ability to do them. Look!" Père Jean extended his hands. "I have two hands", he pointed out to the young brave. "How many have you?"

The brave lifted his hands, scowling. He shrugged. "Two", he said.

"And up here", Père Jean tapped his head. "I have a brain. What have you up there?"

"A brain!"

"If your argument is true, if there are two Gods,

how is it that both of us have exactly two hands and one brain? In truth, the very same God has given us our hands and brains. What we do and make with them is left to us." Père Jean smiled, "Does that answer your question?"

The young brave said he would think it over.

An older Indian, wearing a dirty patch over an eye socket emptied in battle, asked the next question. "This place where good Christians go after death", he inquired. "You call that heaven?"

Père Jean nodded.

"Is there tobacco there? If I go to heaven, can I smoke?"

Again, with great patience, Père Jean explained. The human mind, he told the Indian, cannot imagine the glory that is heaven. "We only know", he said, "that there is a heaven and that those who do God's will on earth eventually get there."

"How far is it from here?" demanded a lean, beady-eyed young man.

"Heaven is on no map", replied Père Jean quickly.

The lean Indian grunted. "When a man is old enough to die", he grumbled, "he's tired. Perhaps your heaven is too far away. Perhaps it is too much of a journey for a tired old man who is almost dead."

The brightly painted brave who had asked the first question spoke again. He would become a

Christian, he said, if all the other members of his
tribe would. "If I were the only one to go to
heaven", he objected, "I would be very lonely.
All my friends would be elsewhere."

And so it went—for many hours; and Père Isaac
marveled at Père Jean's patience. He stored away
in his own mind everything he heard, knowing
that shortly he too would be called on to instruct
the Indians.

The Jesuits were pleased that the Indians visited
the Mission House in such numbers. They were
less pleased that many days some of them lingered
on after dark. This gave them too little time to
recite the office and to talk over their mission prob-
lems.

"Why not just ask them to leave?" Père Isaac
suggested one evening.

Père Jean shook his head. "The Indian laws of
courtesy are very strict", he said. "If you ask an
Indian to leave your house, he will become your
enemy for life."

"All the same", said Isaac, half to himself and
half to Jean Amyot, who was sitting beside him,
"there must be some way to persuade them to go
home at a reasonable hour." A few days later, to
Père Isaac's great delight, little Jean found a way.

Among the Jesuit's few material possessions was
a small clock. The Indians were fascinated by it.
They would stand for minutes, heads bent, listening

to its tireless tick-tock. They often shouted with glee when the little timepiece struck the hour.

They had no notion of machinery. They believed a spirit lived in the clock. It was the spirit, they said, that went "tick-tock" all the time and "ding-ding" on the hour. They asked the priests "What does Captain Clock eat?" and "When does he sleep?"

On the morning that Jean Amyot thought of a polite way of getting the Indians home earlier, Père Isaac was conducting instructions for the first time. He and Jean sat together on a log near the living room fires. Sprawled about the room, contentedly drawing on their pipes, were half a dozen Indians.

As the clock ceased striking the hour of eleven, an old chief addressed Isaac by his Huron name.

"Ondessonk," he said, "every so often, Captain Clock goes 'ding, ding.' Tell me, what is Captain Clock saying?"

Before Père Isaac could think of some pleasant reply, he heard little Jean speaking.

"When Captain Clock strikes twelve times", the boy was telling the Indian, "he is saying, 'Put on the kettle.'"

The Indian grunted. All the other Indians grunted with him and nodded smilingly. "Put on the kettle" meant food, and many of them came to the Mission House because the French were better cooks than their squaws.

"But", little Jean went on hurriedly, "when Captain Clock strikes four times, he is saying, 'Time to go home!' "

"Out of the mouths of babes", thought Père Isaac, trying hard to hide his amusement and wondering what the Indians would say to Jean's words. To his surprise, they again nodded, though not so cheerfully as before. They had great respect for Captain Clock and his invisible spirit. Whatever the captain said must be obeyed. From then on, whenever the clock struck four, the Indians arose and silently departed.

Then the Jesuits chanted their prayers and ate a light supper.

After supper, they talked. They made plans for the Mission. Even now, under Père Jean's direction, another church was going up in a Huron village twelve miles to the south. Soon, they hoped, there would be churches in other Huron towns.

They talked of New France. Only slightly more than a century before, Père Jean reminded them, Jacques Cartier had discovered the Gulf of the Saint Lawrence. On a hill above it, he had planted the fleur-de-lis, the flower which was the royal emblem of France, and claimed this new land for France. Other daring explorers had followed him. In 1608, the brave French soldier, Samuel de Champlain, had founded Quebec. He had pressed far into the wilderness, south to the lake that bore his name, and west to Lake Huron.

Some evenings, the French workmen who lived at the Mission House joined in these talks. One of them had been a fur trapper in his youth. He had traveled far in the New World and talked to many people.

No one, he told the priests, knew yet how large America was. If a man went far enough west, it was thought, he would find a waterway to the rich cities of India. Many Europeans still came to the New World with that in mind. The man who could find a new trade route to the Orient, they reasoned, would make himself and his nation very rich.

Others came to buy furs from the Indians. Still others, though not many yet, came to build homes and settle.

"I hear", said one of the Jesuits, "that the Dutch and the English are founding more and more settlements in the New World."

"I hear the same", said the workman who had once been a fur trapper. "We French must hurry. The nation that brings the most settlers is the nation that will own this great land."

The workman could not look into the future. He had no way of knowing how true his words were. Not too far in the future—in 1759—the French and the English would battle at Quebec. It would be England's victory. Soon after, France would lose all of North America to the English, mostly because England had sent over twenty set-

tlers to every one sent by France. Even England
would not keep all of the New World. In a later
and still more famous war—the American Revolu-
tion of 1776—the independent United States would
be formed.

The Jesuits, sitting around their Mission House
fires in the winter of 1636, could not see the part
they were playing in this great drama of history.
Two centuries later, an American historian would
write that it was these self-sacrificing priests, "toil-
ing to teach a few virtues to the savages", who
opened the doors of the New World to Christianity.

"It is not for us", said Père Jean one evening,
"to hunt for waterways to India. It is not for us
to concern ourselves with buying and selling furs.
Our task is to save the souls of these savages. It
is not an easy task."

The others nodded. Père Jean, they knew, did
not speak out of ignorance. The big, gentle Jesuit
had lived among the Hurons longer than all the
rest of them put together.

"These Indians need our teachings", he told
them. "It is pitiable to see them living in fear of
imaginary demons because they do not know the
mercy of God. It is pitiable to see them dying need-
lessly, because they do not know the rules of good
health.

"In teaching them, remember that we have two
powerful weapons. One is God's grace. The other

is the example we set. We can teach the Indians kindness only by being kind. We can teach them goodness only by being good ourselves. We can teach them love only by loving them."

Père Jean fell silent. The only sound in the Mission House was the hissing of the fires. Père Isaac nodded. Come what may, he promised himself, he would not forget Père Jean's words.

7

THE COMING OF HIM-WHO-
BRINGS-BLESSINGS

I N THE DARK MISSION CABIN, someone was shaking
Père Isaac. He awoke with a start. Late the night
before, he had returned from a five-day journey
to some of the other Huron villages. It took him
a minute to realize that he was home again, that
the freckled face above him belonged to Jean
Amyot.

"Time to get up, *mon Père*", said the boy. "Did
you have a good journey?"

"Very good, Jean. Have you been a good boy?"

"I tried to be", laughed Jean, hurrying on to

the other Jesuits, still asleep on their rough mats on the floor of the Mission House living room.

A second later, the boy was back at Isaac's side. "In honor of Advent", he told Père Isaac, "Père Jean wrote a Christmas carol while you were away. He's taught it to some of the Indian children. They're practicing here today. I hope you get a chance to hear them."

"I'll try to be here, Jean."

It was in the afternoon, just before the early winter darkness, that Père Jean instructed the Indian children. When Père Isaac slipped into the living room, the children were already gathered around the fires.

He found a place by Jean Amyot, and returned the little French boy's happy wink.

Père Jean strode into the room, and the Indian children shouted "*Shay!*" It was their expression for "Hello and welcome!"

Père Jean responded. Then he began the instructions.

There was no word in the Huron language for God. There was no word for Christ. Père Jean had taught the children to speak of God in their own tongue as "Him-Who-Made-the-World". He had taught them to speak of Christ as "Him-Who-Brings-Blessings".

Père Jean blessed himself. The children did the same. Some were not quite sure how to do it.

Their little brown hands flew every which way like a cat's tail. They giggled and nudged one another.

Père Jean said the Our Father and the Hail Mary. He had translated them into Huron poetry. He paused after each phrase, and the children repeated it.

Then he told them the great story. Once upon a time, he told them, a powerful chief ordered Our Lady and Saint Joseph to go from their village to a larger village called Bethlehem. In Bethlehem there was no room for them in the cabins where the people slept. They had to spend the night in the horses' cabin. And there Him-Who-Brings-Blessings was born.

Père Isaac looked around the semicircle. The children's eyes were shining. Not a hand stirred. He felt a tug at his cassock. "Now!" whispered Jean Amyot. "Now! They're going to sing the carol!"

Père Jean had lifted his hand. He hummed a note. The Indian children had good ears. They swung easily into the simple melody. The little French boy, already a master of the Huron language, sang with them. In a swelling shiver of sound the light voices blended in the second and third stanzas:

> Within a lodge of broken bark
> > the tender babe was found,
> A ragged robe of rabbit skin
> > enwrapped his beauty round.

And as the hunter braves drew nigh,
The angel song rang loud and high:
Jeous Ahatonhia!
Jesus, our King, is born!
The earliest moon of winter time
is not so round and fair
As was the ring of glory on
the helpless infant there.
While chiefs from far before him knelt,
With gifts of fox and beaver pelt.
Jeous Ahatonhia!
Jesus, our King, is born!
In Excelsis Gloria!

Père Isaac listened with pleasure. These copper-skinned children sitting here on the rim of civilization—and singing a Christmas carol. Could anything, thought Isaac, be more wonderful than that?

8

FLAMING MAGIC

THE JESUITS HOPED that with the coming of cold weather, the sickness raging through the Huron villages would die out. Instead it increased. It was a strong and often fatal kind of influenza. Père Jean, returning to the Mission House from a tour of the villages, brought grim news.

"Everywhere", he said, "the Indians are dying, dying. Everywhere, they are turning to their medicine men."

Often when an Indian found he had no skill as a hunter or a fisherman or a warrior, he set himself up as a medicine man or sorcerer. He claimed to be on friendly terms with a powerful spirit. He claimed to be able to cure the sick with his magic.

In the late winter of 1637, the medicine men were active in all the Huron villages. They commanded the people to perform weird ceremonies. There were Eat-All feasts. For hours on end, the Indians sat around steaming kettles and gorged themselves.

"It is sad, sad", said Père Jean, "to see these poor people trying to make themselves well by eating themselves sick."

There were grotesque rites. All the Indians gathered in a large longhouse. The braves danced like madmen. They stuffed red-hot coals in their mouths. They grabbed burning brands and flung them here and there. Their frightened squaws ran about putting out fires lest their fragile cabins go up in flames. Sometimes a medicine man danced around the mat of a sick person. He shouted and shrieked. At his bidding the other Indians in the cabin did the same.

"If a person were not already ill", sighed Père Jean, "such a frightful racket would surely make him ill."

Once, visiting a cabin, Père Isaac witnessed a ceremony he would never forget. He was standing by the mat of a sick brave when one of the medicine men rushed in.

The medicine man was a slender, angular Indian

with protruding teeth. On each upper arm he wore a huge tattoo representing the sun, an effect he had gotten by painting his flesh with a mixture of charcoal and the juice of wild berries.

With a growl, he thrust Père Isaac aside. "Blackrobe's magic no good here", he snarled. "Sick man has demon in him. My magic will draw demon out of sick man. Look!"

And the medicine man began to dance. Around and around the sick man's mat, he danced. Around and around, until Isaac's head swam, watching him. Around and around, screaming and shrieking, his moccasined feet pounding the dusty floor.

Suddenly, swooping down, he bit the sick man's cheek, drawing blood. Whirling around the head of the man, he dipped and bit the other cheek, again drawing blood. Then, jumping to his feet, he lifted his right arm, his fist closed, and uttered a cry of triumph.

"Behold!" he shouted. "My magic has drawn the demon out of the sick man. Behold, the demon that was in him is now in my hand!"

And with that, the sweating medicine man opened his lifted palm, displaying a small piece of animal bone inside.

The other Indians in the cabin gasped, convinced that the bone was indeed a demon. They were amazed. Père Isaac wasn't. Describing the incident to Père Jean later, he shook his head sadly.

"As far as I know," he said, "not one Indian saw what I saw. The medicine man had that bone in his mouth when he entered the cabin. I saw the bulge in his cheek. I also saw him spit it into his hand just before he lifted his arm and showed it to the people."

Foremost among the medicine men was a misshapen little Indian known as the Hunchback. This man, the Jesuits learned, was going from town to town in the Huron country. Wherever he stopped, there were frenzied ceremonies, sometimes lasting for days. One wind-lashed winter evening, he appeared in the living room of the Mission House.

The Jesuits were in the chapel. The sickness had struck the Mission House itself. For several days, Jean Amyot had been confined to his mat in the living room. To fervent prayers for all the stricken Hurons, the priests added special prayers for Jean. Suddenly, they heard a piercing scream in the other room; and another, and another, each higher than the last, like the whinnying of a horse in pain.

Hurrying into the living room, they found the Hunchback standing near the front door. They knew him at once, from descriptions some of the Indians had given them. A bony, twisted little man, his whole body was streaked with bright, greasy paints. In his upheld hands were two objects that Père Isaac, straining to see in the shadowy room, could not at first make out.

As the Jesuits came in, the Hunchback leaned back like a howling dog, uttering still another series of unearthly screams. He stepped into the light of the fires. Now Isaac could see the objects he carried. One clawlike hand held a large turkey wing. The other gripped the handle of a small iron kettle.

"Blackrobes!" he shouted. "Who is captain here?"

Père Jean stepped forward. "I am the Superior", he said. "What can we do for you?"

"Ah!" The Hunchback laughed. "You cannot do anything for me. I come to do something for you." He pointed the turkey wing at Jean Amyot, who, lying on his mat in a dark corner, watched the scene with fascinated eyes. "One of your own people is sick", the Hunchback went on. "I was told the boy was ill, and I came quickly to offer you a magic cure for him. Look!" He extended the kettle toward Père Jean. "Magic cure. Made according to a great spirit's directions. Good magic that only I can make. Quick magic that never fails. Look!"

Père Jean looked into the kettle, wrinkling his nose. "It stinks!" he said to the other Jesuits, speaking in French.

Père Isaac stepped forward. The kettle contained some sort of melted animal fat. The grease was rancid and black with filth.

"I dip my turkey wing into this", cried the

Hunchback. "I brush the body of the sick child—
once, twice, three times!" The Hunchback's voice
rose higher and higher, becoming a wail. "Once—
twice—three times, I brush him, and behold he is
well!"

He drew closer to Père Jean, lowering his voice
to a husky whisper. "I do not ask much for it.
Only three things."

He looked slowly around the room.

"That!" he cried suddenly, pointing to a small
hand grain mill that one of the priests had brought
out from Three Rivers.

The Hunchback's eyes roamed again. They were
needle sharp and greedy. "And that!" he screamed
suddenly, pointing to Captain Clock, standing on
a small table near Jean's mat. "And one thing more
that I was told was here but which I do not see."

"Just a minute", said Père Jean. "Are you offering
to sell us your magic?"

"I only ask three things for it: that!" The Hunchback pointed again to the grain mill. "And Captain
Clock! And one more thing that I was told was
here but which I do not see." He drew still closer
to Père Jean. "The cup!" he screamed. "Where do
you keep your golden cup?"

"Someone", said Père Isaac, "has told him about
the chalice on the altar."

Père Jean shook his head in the Hunchback's face.
"We will not buy anything from you", he said.

"When we are ill, we ask God's help. We do not believe in magic."

"But this magic is good!" cried the Hunchback, suddenly darting to Jean Amyot's mat and dipping his turkey wing into the filthy grease. His object, apparently, was to brush the child with the grease and so show the priests that the magic worked. Before he could do so, Père Jean had crossed the room. He grabbed the kneeling Hunchback by the arm and dragged him to his feet.

"Do not touch the child!" he thundered. Père Isaac had never seen his Superior angry before. Père Jean's big frame shook. His voice, ordinarily so gentle, filled the room. His eyes flashed. "I have never asked an Indian to leave this place before", he shouted. "But I ask you now. Get out! You are a mischief-maker. You are a cheat and a fraud! *Get out!*"

The Hunchback stood, close to the Jesuit Superior. His sharp eyes shifted from face to face around the room, returning finally to Père Jean. With a quick snap of his head, he spat, full in the priest's face, turned on his heel and went out.

Père Jean's head dropped. "God forgive me", he murmured. "I did not mean to lose my temper."

"No one could blame you", said Isaac, hurrying over to see that young Jean was all right. "I hope we have seen the last of the Hunchback."

"I am much afraid", said Père Jean, "that we have seen only the beginning of him."

Père Jean was right. A few days later, Jean Amyot, fully recovered from his long illness, came into the Mission House to tell the priests that the Hunchback was leading a big procession through the crooked village streets. The Jesuits hurried out to watch.

A throng of young braves followed the medicine man. "The Hunchback is about to undergo a three-day sweat", one of them kept shouting. In this way he is going to drive out the Spirit-Who-Causes-the-Pestilence."

Outside the village palisades, squaws leaned three tall poles against each other and lashed them together. They wrapped strips of bark around the poles. Into this lodge they carried heated rocks, filling it with smoke.

The Hunchback threw a heavy robe around his shoulders and entered the lodge. For three days he sweated there. He took neither food nor water. From time to time, he could be heard crying:

"Go away, Spirit-Who-Causes-the-Pestilence. Leave our villages! If you must eat flesh, go eat the flesh of our enemies, the Iroquois!"

On the morning of the third day, all the Indians gathered around the "sweat lodge". Inside, the Hunchback threw off his heavy robe. With a shriek,

he flung a handful of tobacco on the hot rocks.
As the flames leaped, he once again shouted:
"Go away, Spirit-Who-Causes-the-Pestilence!
Leave our villages!"
Then he emerged from the lodge. He faced the
crowd, a greasy, thin, gaudy figure. His magic
had worked, he told them. By nightfall the village
would be free of sickness.
That day, the little town was wrapped in silence.
Père Isaac, visiting the sick, found the Indians hud-
dled around their fires, tense and waiting.
Nightfall came. Now, according to the Hunch-
back's boast, the pestilence would go away. But
it didn't. More Indians fell sick. By morning, still
more infants had died. Everywhere he went,
throughout the day, Père Isaac heard the Indians
muttering.
"The Hunchback's magic has failed", some said.
"The Hunchback has deceived us", said others.
And some growled, "The Hunchback must die!"
When Isaac reported these things to Père Jean,
the big Jesuit shook his head thoughtfully.
"Will they kill the Hunchback?" asked Isaac.
"They may", said Père Jean. "Unless . . . !"
"Unless what?"
"Unless he can think of some trick to stop them."
Early the next morning, Père Isaac entered a cabin
to visit a sick baby. He found the smoke-filled

room crowded with silent and dejected Indians. He gave the child a little warm broth. He had brought a portion of the Jesuits' dwindling stock of dried figs and raisins. He had thought he would leave a couple of these precious treats behind; but a close look at the little one's wizened face told him it would be useless. The boy was dying.

He got a cup of water. The child's mother was sitting beside him, her eyes on the floor. She had not lifted them once since Isaac's arrival. He tried to attract her attention. It was no use. Taking her silence as a sign of consent, he made ready to baptize the dying baby.

As he did so, the woman leaped to her feet, shrieking at him. Her cries aroused the others. Père Isaac found himself surrounded by a swarm of gesturing and angrily screaming savages.

Their words were violent, swift. For the life of him he could not make out what they were saying. He only knew that he had no choice but to leave.

In the Mission House that night, he learned that the other priests had encountered similar hostility in the Indian cabins. Père Jean, alarmed, sent for a friendly village chief.

When the Indian arrived, he listened carefully to the priests' stories.

"Blackrobes", he said. "I will speak plainly. The Hunchback is to blame for this. He promised to get rid of the sickness and he failed. Yesterday, many of the villagers were angry. Some threatened to take his life. To save his skin, the Hunchback is saying that his magic will not work because your magic is stronger."

"But we have no magic", protested Père Jean. "You know we have no magic."

"I know it", said the chief. "And you know it. But many of my people are a little foolish in their heads. This pestilence has made them even more foolish. They are distracted. They are ready to believe anything!"

The tall chieftain took a deep breath. "Take my advice", he said. "Do not leave your house for a few days. Do not visit the Indian cabins. Many of the villagers are convinced that you are sorcerers. They are convinced that this sickness will not go until you are dead!"

Père Jean thanked the chief, who grunted his farewell and left.

Isaac was the first to speak. "But if we do not visit the Indian cabins, we cannot do our work."

"We will visit them", said Père Jean. "We will go on just as we always have."

The other Jesuits nodded. All agreed that this was the course they must follow.

At supper, the workmen who lived with them offered to take turns standing watch during the night.

Père Jean shook his head. "Tomorrow is going to be a hard day", he said. "We will all need our rest. I ask only one thing of each of you: before you retire, say an extra prayer for these unhappy savages."

9

PÈRE JEAN'S FEAST

FOR MONTHS THE JESUITS worked with the threat of death hanging over them. Shouted taunts and insults followed Père Isaac as he tramped the frozen streets.

Once, as he passed a cabin, a young brave charged out. He grabbed Père Isaac and hurled the Jesuit to his knees. For fully a minute, the infuriated Indian stood over Isaac, his tomahawk raised and poised to strike.

"Why he did not kill me then and there," Isaac told Père Jean that evening, "why he simply turned after a while and walked away, I do not know."

"Were you calm, Isaac?"

"What else could I be under the circumstances?"

"Perhaps that explains it. These Indians admire bravery. Had you shown the slightest fear, you might not be with us now."

Spring came early to the Huron country, with pale green leaves curling like limp rags along the oak tree limbs. The first summer days were hot and cloudless, followed by a July of soaking rains and a sultry August.

In the drowsy stillness of an autumn afternoon, Père Isaac and another of the Fathers sat in the Mission House living room. Few Indians visited the Mission these days. Even Captain Clock was still. Word had reached the priests that some Hurons thought the spirit that went "tick-tock" inside the clock was the cause of the sickness. On the advice of a friendly Indian, the Jesuits had let the little clock run down.

Père Isaac and his companion were reading the office. Suddenly the street outside, and soon the room itself, shook with sound. A mob of brawling warriors poured in. A glance told Père Isaac that they were not of this village. They came from another Huron town.

Their chief was a wiry, grotesquely tattooed man. He came at once to Isaac.

"You blackrobes are sorcerers", he bellowed. "Your spirits sow the sickness that destroys our people!"

By this time, all the other braves had crowded

into the chapel behind them. Isaac could hear them there, snorting among themselves. Throughout the day, the chapel was open to the Indians, but these men, Isaac realized, had never been in it before.

The tattooed chieftain took a position near the street door. He placed an arrow in his bow and drew back the bow string.

He hesitated, apparently undecided as to which of the Jesuits to kill first. Suddenly, the muted muttering in the next room swelled to a shattering clamor. The tattooed chief looked from the Jesuits to the chapel door and back. He was torn between a desire to kill Isaac and his companion at once, and curiosity about what was happening in the next room.

Curiosity won. Lowering his bow, the chief sprinted into the little chapel.

Père Isaac followed as far as the open door. He saw at once what had excited the Indians.

It was the holy pictures. The braves were running wildly from one to another, from Christ to Our Lady and then to Saint Joseph.

"These must be the blackrobes' spirits!" he heard one shout.

And from another:

"We must ask the chief men of the village what these mean!"

Père Isaac stepped back as the Indians stampeded from the chapel, through the living room and into the dusty street. In a few seconds, street and Mission House were once again emptied of sound.

The two Jesuits exchanged glances.

"The good Lord has saved us", said Isaac's companion, and Père Isaac nodded.

On a brooding October evening, a chief from another village entered the Mission House living room. He announced that he had something to say to all the Jesuits. He was a rugged, handsome man. The priests addressed him as Joseph, for during the summer he had been baptized and had taken a Christian name.

"Fathers", Joseph began, after the priests had assembled. "I bring you troubling news. Soon delegates from all four Huron nations will meet here in solemn council. Perhaps you have heard about this council. Perhaps you know its purpose."

Père Jean nodded. "Yes, yes, Joseph", he said. "We know that at this council our fate will be decided. The chiefs and ancients will vote on whether we live or die."

"That is right", said Joseph. "I must go on an errand far from here. I will not be at the council fire to plead your case. You must speak for yourselves. I beg of you—be prepared to plead your case well!"

One evening, later in October, the Indian delegates gathered in the town's largest longhouse. They sat around a single fire, crouching on the dirt floor or on the platforms along either wall.

Every speaker began in the same way. "Close your mouths and open your ears", he sang out in the high council pitch. Each ended with the same expression, "*Hiro!*" meaning "I have spoken."

The Jesuits, seated in a corner of the room, listened carefully to the charges against them.

One ancient declared that the influenza epidemic was caused by a "corpse" which the priests kept hidden in their chapel. His ringing *Hiro!* was still echoing through the cabin when Père Jean got to his feet.

"My friends," he said, "there is indeed a Body on the altar of our chapel. It is the Body of Him-Who-Brings-Blessings. We have told you about this. But instead of listening with both ears, you have listened with only one. You have misunderstood us. Know then that this Body you speak of is the Blessed Sacrament. It is not a dead thing, but a living one. It brings harm to no man and good to all."

The Indians heard him out politely for that was their way. When he had finished, another chief spoke.

"The Spirit-Who-Causes-the-Sickness", he asserted, "lives far from here. How then does he know where the Huron country is? He knows because the blackrobes mark the spot. They mark the spot with that little black rag at the top of the fir tree next to their cabin!"

Again, patiently, Père Jean answered the Indians.

"My friends," he said, "that little black rag on the fir tree by the Mission House is no signal. It is a weather vane. We put it there to tell the direction of the wind."

Next, Père Isaac spoke. "We grieve for you", he told the Indians. "We pray for you constantly. But the sickness cannot be stopped by chasing away spirits that do not exist. Forget your spirits—and clean your cabins. Forget your charms and ceremonies—and clean your bodies. Strain the grease from your broths and drink only the healthy essences."

Père Isaac spoke, as all the others did, in the high council pitch. "Lately", he intoned, "some of you have barred your doors against us. Open them again. Let us come to you. Let us share with you our broths and our raisins and our prunes."

Late at night, the council broke up. No decision had been reached. The next night a second council was held. This time the Jesuits were not permitted to attend; but they sat outside, close enough to hear the speeches.

Toward morning, a friendly Indian emerged from the longhouse. He was shaking his head. "Fathers," he told the priests sadly, "you are dead men."

"But no decision has been reached", protested Père Jean.

"There will be no official decision", said the Huron. "The chiefs are afraid to condemn you officially. They are afraid of offending the French and of losing their trading rights. I happen to know, however, that they spoke with some young braves of the village this afternoon. Unofficially, they gave the young men permission to kill you."

At noon, the following day, Père Jean assembled the Jesuits in the Mission House living room.

"As I have often told you," he said, "when an Indian knows that his people are going to kill him, he gives a farewell feast. In this way he shows that he is not afraid to die. Tonight, we are giving a farewell feast. A messenger is going through the village now. I have invited all the important Indians."

The feast started early and lasted far into the night. Each red-skinned guest, as he came in, was escorted to a place by the Mission fires. The Jesuits served him. Baked squash, smoked fish and venison were placed before him. Steaming *sagamite*, a sort of corn mush, was ladled out of the smoking kettles.

Each guest ate in silence, his expression one of glum hostility. As he departed, he paused briefly at the door and grunted the Huron word for "thanks".

Midway in the evening, the friendly Indian called

Père Jean aside. "This is a wise thing you have done", he told the Jesuit Superior. "I have been talking with the young braves in the village. They are pleased with your courage. Your lives may be saved yet."

"And yet", said Père Jean with a smile, "they may not be."

The Indian nodded solemnly. "True", he agreed, "and yet they may not be."

Although the feast lasted late, the Jesuits said Mass and breakfasted at their usual hour in the morning. Dawn was still purple in the streets when Père Isaac set out on his daily calls.

He went first to a cabin where he knew many were ill. For weeks, this cabin had been closed to him. This morning, however, no Indian stood on the narrow porch, barring his way.

Père Isaac sighed. This could mean that all was well. It could also mean that the Indian was lurking just inside the door, waiting to lower his tomahawk.

With a whispered prayer, the young Jesuit shoved aside the stiff deerskin over the opening. In the thick and musty smoke of the interior, a score of Indians moved about the fires, preparing breakfast. Isaac made his way to a dark corner where an old squaw lay dying.

He half expected the woman to cover her head with the blanket, as had happened many times lately in other cabins. When nothing of the sort occurred,

he filled the woman's bowl with broth. He held
her hands while she guided it, tremblingly, to her
lips.

He went to the others who were sick. The beady
eyes, looking up from the mats, were friendly.
His heart sang. He felt somehow that the danger
had passed. "Père Jean's feast", he told himself,
"has worked!"

10

JEAN AMYOT BECOMES RICH

A FEW DAYS LATER, as Père Isaac left an Indian cabin, he heard his name called. It was one of the workmen from the Mission House. "Père Jean wishes to see you", he told Isaac. "He says come at once. It's important."

"What now?" Isaac wondered. Winter had come, and the hard-packed snow of the streets crackled under his boots as he hurried toward the Mission House.

In the living room, Père Jean was talking to a young Indian couple. On the woman's back, on a cradle board held by a strap across the forehead, rested a sleeping baby.

"Ah, Isaac", said Père Jean, as Isaac came in. "You remember my speaking of a young couple in one of the other villages. I baptized them in their home a month ago."

Isaac nodded. "Are these the people?"

"Yes", said Père Jean. "For the last few days, they have been visiting relatives here. They have seen a great deal of Jean Amyot. They have taken a liking to the boy. They would like to take him into their home."

Père Isaac looked again at the Indians. The man had a firm, forthright look. The woman's eyes were large and soft; she was very pretty.

"Under what conditions do they want the boy?" asked Père Isaac.

"They wish to adopt him. They would like to bring him up as their own son. What do you say?"

"I don't know what to say", said Isaac.

"We would all miss him", Père Jean seemed to read Isaac's thoughts. "But in the home of this Indian couple, Jean would be safe."

"He's safe here."

"Now, yes. For the time being, we are in the good graces of the Indians. But you know as well as I do, Isaac, that this can change any minute. Another pestilence, a drought next summer—any trouble, and the Hurons' anger may fall on us again. On the other hand, once the boy is adopted by these people", Père Jean nodded toward the Indians, "he will be considered a full-fledged member of the tribe. No Huron will ever lift a hand against him."

Père Isaac sighed deeply. "Has the boy been told of this?"

Père Jean shook his head. "You are closer to him than any of us. I thought perhaps you would speak to him."

The Indian couple departed. Père Isaac waited until after the noon meal. Then, taking a small book from among his belongings, he called to Jean to come outside with him.

They walked through one of the village gates, and took the path across the snow-covered clearing and into the woods. A few feet within the forest, some spruce trees formed a natural grove. Here, on a tree trunk, Père Isaac had carved a cross. Many times, he and Jean, alone or with some of the other priests, had come here to pray.

Entering the grove, the priest and the boy dropped to their knees. Jean took a rosary from his pocket.

Père Isaac began: "I believe in God, the Father Almighty, Creator of heaven and earth . . ."

The boy's smaller voice kept pace with his. Père Isaac announced the mystery of the Annunciation.

"Hail, Mary, full of grace . . ."

When they had finished the Rosary, Père Isaac opened the small book in his hand. From Three

Rivers, he had been able to bring only four books: his breviary, a small missal, a copy of the *Spiritual Exercises* by the founder of his Order and this well-thumbed copy of the *Imitation of Christ* by Thomas à Kempis. He motioned the boy to a nearby log, and opened the little volume at random.

"When thou hast Christ," he read, "thou art rich and hath enough. He will be thy faithful and provident helper in all things, so thou shalt not need to trust in men. For these are . . ."

Père Isaac broke off, aware that the lad was staring at him in a peculiar way.

"*Mon Père*," said the boy, "you have something on your mind."

Isaac closed the book. "Yes, Jean", he said. "An Indian couple wish to take you to their home."

"To live with them, Père Isaac?"

"Yes. They want to adopt you. They're leaving in the morning."

"Leaving? These people do not live in our village?"

"No, in one of the other towns. But that won't matter, Jean. You know how much we travel. Every time I come to your town, I'll see you."

The boy's eyes searched the ground. It hurt Père Isaac to notice how suddenly solemn the small, freckled face had become.

"Do I have to go?" asked Jean.

"No", said Père Isaac. "Père Jean says the decision is up to you."

"Do you and Père Jean want me to go?"

"We think it would be best for you. The Indians who have asked for you are Christians. They are fine people. They will be good to you. They have children of their own. You will have many playmates. Most important, you will become a citizen of the Huron nation with all the rights and privileges."

Seeing that none of these statements was having any effect on the boy, Père Isaac searched his mind for something else. "Jean," he said, "suppose I were to ask you to do this in the name of your patron, Saint Joseph?"

The boy hung his head. "You know that I could never refuse anything asked in his name."

The Indian couple came to Mass at the Mission the next morning and received Holy Communion. Then they went outside and waited for Jean. The priests and the French workmen helped the lad get his things together.

Jean went about his preparations in silence, his young face set and grim. Not until the last minute did he break, suddenly leaning against the cabin wall, his shoulders shaking.

Hastily, Père Isaac went to the box containing his own few belongings. He pulled out the battered copy of the *Imitation of Christ*. Hurrying to Jean, he placed it in one of his hands.

The boy straightened, his face working. He looked at the book, then at Père Isaac. "But, *mon*

Père," he protested. "I've often heard you say—
this book is very precious to you."

"What would be the sense of giving you something", said Isaac, "that wasn't precious to me?
That book has been a good friend to me, Jean. It
will be a good friend to you."

Again the lad's eyes went from book to priest.
He sniffled a few times, and then broke into a half
grin.

"Get along with you now", cried Père Isaac,
opening the door and giving Jean Amyot a gentle
shove. "Read the *Imitation* and don't forget your
prayers!"

The other Jesuits and the workmen had crowded
into the doorway. They watched as Jean and his
new foster-parents trudged down the snow-bright
street. They watched until the boy and the Indians
had vanished down the road.

II

A WILD JOURNEY

T HE JESUITS WERE NOT BOTHERED by the medicine
men that winter. Many Hurons still regarded
them as sorcerers, but many more welcomed them
into their cabins.

Little by little the Mission House living room
became once again a scene of daily religious instructions. By the fall of 1639, the Fathers could count
at least a hundred adult converts. Peter, the first
such convert, had died, but the Jesuits heard that
his widow—living in a village to the east—was
bringing up her children according to the simple
laws of God. They heard similar reports of Joseph,

the convert chief who had come to their aid during the epidemic of the year before.

Late fall brought driving rains. Chill winds promised an early winter. One afternoon, Père Jean gathered the Jesuits around the Mission House fires. His face was grave. In one hand he held a rolled-up parchment.

"We are established here now", he began, after the Fathers had seated themselves. "The time has come for us to carry the Word of God still farther into the wilderness. I am going to ask two of you to visit the Tobacco People. You know the tribe I mean. They speak the same language as our people here and live in the same manner. If you find them friendly, stay awhile, perhaps all winter. If not, you will know what to do."

Père Jean unrolled the parchment in his hand and spread it on the dirt floor of the cabin.

"This map", he explained, "was drawn by a fur trader. This is the Huron country." Taking a charred stick from the fire, Père Jean drew a circle around the broad peninsula stretching into Lake Huron. "Down here", and he shifted the stick, "is the country of the Tobacco People. It is a wild country. There are high mountains, raging streams, dangerous swamps. In this country even an experienced woodsman could easily lose his way."

Père Jean's voice trailed away, to be replaced by the sputter-sputter of the fires dampened by the rain falling through the Mission House roof.

Père Isaac had got to his feet. "In other words," he said, "you are asking for volunteers."

"I could not bring myself", said Père Jean, "to order anyone to make this trip. The men who go on this journey may never return."

"I would be glad to go", said Isaac.

"And I!" The priest who spoke was Père Charles Garnier. Père Charles was a frail man, so shy that he almost always blushed when spoken to. At thirty, he was still beardless. He himself made a joke of it, often saying, "What a great baby I am." But the Indians loved him for it. They too were beardless. They considered Père Charles much the handsomest of the Jesuit Fathers. They called him *Ouracha*, meaning "Beautiful".

After Mass the next morning, Isaac and Charles made their preparations. Each tucked up his black robes and bound on buckskin leggings and heavy boots. They drew skin coats over their cassocks and put on fur caps. About their shoulders they strapped blankets and clothes, equipment for Mass and bags full of beads, knives and awls to be distributed as gifts among the Indians. At his side, each priest strung his snowshoes, his breviary and his food bags.

Thus equipped, they set forth. It was a dull, wet day. The heavy rains had left the paths slippery and hard to follow. By nightfall, traveling without food or rest, they had reached the southernmost Huron town.

Their plan was to spend the night with Joseph, the Christian chief.

"Perhaps", said Père Charles, "Joseph will be willing to travel with us as our guide."

"If not," Père Isaac replied, "we will ask him to find us someone else."

The village streets were almost deserted. Inquiring at the first cabin, Père Isaac learned that Joseph had long since left the longhouse where he and his wife had once lived with other Indian families. They lived now, he was told, in a cabin of their own.

It was the most unusual Indian cabin Père Isaac had seen. He and Père Charles gasped as they stepped in. "What a difference a knowledge of cleanliness makes in the everyday lives of these Indians," he thought; for Joseph's cabin was as clean as the Mission House. The cooking utensils, carefully scrubbed, hung on pegs along the walls. A partition split the building into two small but neatly arranged rooms. Already, although the season of Advent was not yet at hand, Joseph's children had built a small crèche of cedar wood. Under a crucifix attached to one of the posts stood a crude prayer stand.

Maria, Joseph's pretty young wife, was alone in the front room. Seated by the fires, she was braiding strands of elm bark, to make a large fishing net for her husband to carry to the lake the next summer.

She greeted the priests with a low bow. Proudly she summoned her children, three strapping boys and a small girl.

"Joseph is meeting with the chieftains," she said, "but he will be with us soon."

She spread a mat before the fire and motioned the priests to be seated. She threw ears of corn and squash into the embers and ladled smoking sagamite into earthenware bowls. They were still eating when Joseph appeared.

"News of your arrival reached me in the village", he told them. "I have informed the other Christians. They will join us this evening."

But his smile faded when the priests told him their mission. "You go among the Tobacco People?" he demanded. "Could you not put off your journey until summer?"

Père Isaac shook his head. "In summer," he pointed out, "the braves are on the trail. We go at this season, because now we can carry the gospel to all."

"But you will not find the Tobacco People friendly."

"Why do you say that?"

"Because most of them consider you evil sorcerers, just as many Hurons still do."

"We are not afraid of the people," said Isaac, "but we know very little about their country. We badly need a guide, Joseph. We would be most happy if you would travel with us."

Joseph did not answer immediately. His eyes went to his wife. At a nod from him, she led the children into the other room.

"I do not wish the young ones to hear this", explained Joseph. "You see how we live now. I built this house, so that we could be by ourselves. I did not want my children listening all day to the superstitious talk of some of the other Indians. Here they can live a Christian life in a clean and orderly home."

The big Indian sighed. "But living this way raises a problem, as you can see", he added. "If there were other families living with us, I would not hesitate to go with you. But to leave my family alone, with the harsh winter setting in—! Oh, my Fathers!" And Joseph spread his arms in a gesture of despair. "You tear my heart in two. One half says, 'Go, for these are your priests, your spiritual fathers.' But the other half says, 'What of your family? Where does your duty lie?' "

"Your duty lies here", said Père Isaac quickly. "Perhaps some other Indian will accompany us."

The big chief shook his head. "Take my word for it, no one will go. No one. Fathers, do not make this journey. Spend the winter with us."

"We have no choice, Joseph", said Père Isaac. "We feel it is our duty to go."

"Then I am afraid you must make the trip alone."

"Those who travel with Christ", Père Charles put in, "are never alone."

That evening the other Christian Indians of the village came to Joseph's cabin. All squatted on the hard floor. Joseph lighted the pipe of friendship at the fires and passed it to the priests. Each took a lingering puff and passed it on. Then the priests retired to the other room and, two at a time, the Indians went in to make their confessions.

At dawn the next morning the two little rooms were filled as Père Isaac laid his altar stone on the prayer stand and offered the Holy Sacrifice of the Mass. Outside a howling wind blew. Twice the single candle on the makeshift altar went out. Père Charles relit it.

After Mass, Joseph led his fellow Christians as they renewed aloud their baptismal vows. Their strong, clear voices rang with faith. As he listened, Isaac knew that he and Charles could not have a more precious farewell gift than this.

The visiting Indians left, and the priests made ready to go. At the last minute, drawing a rough map on the floor with his finger, Joseph showed them the easiest route to the capital town of the Tobacco People.

It was a week's journey, much of it along narrow mountain trails. The first snows came, driven by beating winds. Often, at nightfall, it was all the Jesuits could do to find enough dry wood for a fire. Twice they came to small villages. They found the Tobacco People sullen and suspicious. At each

place, however, they were given food and a place
to sleep.

The capital town lay in a broad valley, its stout
walls surrounded by a moat. They went at once
to the cabin of an important chief. He let them
come in, but there was no pleasure in his eyes as
he pointed to a mat by the fire.

A squaw served them and showed them a corner
where they could spend the night. There were no
sleeping mats for them. Collecting what twigs he
could find in the cabin, each Jesuit made a thin
mattress for himself. Over this he lay his skin coat
and his blankets.

His bed ready, Père Isaac knelt to say his prayers.
He had no sooner blessed himself than a scream
rang through the cabin. A second later, shouting
Indians surrounded the priests.

The chief, squeezing through the noisy crowd,
grabbed Isaac roughly.

"Blackrobes will make no magic here", he
stormed. "We are not ignorant. We have heard
how you brought sickness to the Huron people.
Blackrobes will take their belongings and go!"

The priests had no choice. Out in the snow-swept
streets, they went from cabin to cabin. Everywhere
it was the same story. Runners from the chief's
house had been there before them. At long last,
in a large longhouse near the palisades, a young
brave admitted them.

"My people are being stupid and cruel", he said. "You may take shelter here tonight. But, I beseech you, be gone by morning."

He led them to two mats underneath one of the platforms. The other Indians watched them with frowning eyes, muttering among themselves—all but one, a toothless old woman. Raising herself on her elbow, she beckoned to Père Isaac.

"I am the mother of the brave who invited you in", she told him. "We have relatives in the Huron country, Christian relatives. They visit us; they have spoken of your beliefs—beliefs that I am sure are good and true. Myself, I have only a little while to live. I ask of you, show me the way to heaven."

For hours Père Isaac sat by the old woman's mat, talking to her in whispers. It pleased him to see some of the other Indians edge closer and listen. Toward morning, he baptized the old woman, her son and her son's wife and children.

The Jesuits left the cabin while it was still dark. The Indian town slept as they hurried through the snow-thick streets, through one of the palisades gates, and across a clearing into the protection of the forest.

For more than a week, they wandered.. They stopped at several villages, only to discover that news of their trouble in the capital town had preceded them. No cabins were opened to them. Even their requests for food were refused. Lost and bewildered, they asked for directions to the Huron country. The Indians answered them with silence—and sneers.

One night, camping in a grove of fir trees half way up a mountainside, they looked over their dwindling supplies.

"Enough corn bread for another day, maybe two", said Père Charles grimly. "And that is all."

That night, as usual, they took turns, one tending the fire while the other slept. Shortly after dawn, shouts awakened Père Isaac. Crawling with Charles to the edge of the grove, he saw a band of Indians clambering up the hill. They were armed with bows and spears.

"Warriors!" said Père Charles. "I am afraid these men come to kill us, Isaac."

Isaac nodded. Lifting himself to his knees, he prayed for calmness and courage. Père Charles knelt beside him.

Then Isaac heard his Indian name, "Ondessonk!" He scrambled to his feet, for the voice was a familiar one. He watched, hardly believing his eyes, as the familiar figure detached itself from the oncoming group and came half-running, half-crawling up the snow-covered slope.

"Joseph!" exclaimed Isaac. "How is it you—how is it you are here?"

"News of your trouble reached us days ago", cried Joseph, reaching them and flinging his big arms around the shivering priest. "We have been searching for you since."

"But your family, Joseph. Your wife and children! You have left them alone."

"It was my wife who insisted that I do this. When we heard what had happened to you, neither of us could sleep. But come. We have food. You shall eat. Then we'll see that you get safely home again."

Isaac turned to Père Charles and found the other Jesuit's eyes, like his own, damp with relief and gratitude.

"Those who travel with Christ", said Père Charles, echoing the words he had spoken in Joseph's cabin five weeks before, "are never alone. It is obvious that God has further work for us on this earth."

12

AMBUSH!

TWELVE SLENDER CANOES glided through the
choppy waters of Lake Saint Peter, the wide
section of the Saint Lawrence some leagues west
of Three Rivers. The hot sun of a late August afternoon flamed along the western horizon.

Père Isaac sat behind the steersman in the foremost canoe. The short paddle in his hand raced
through the water as though it were an extension
of his arm. Long living in the wilderness had taught
Isaac many things. He could maneuver a canoe
now as artfully as any copper-skinned voyageur.

Two months before, after six years in the Huron

country, he had made the downstream journey to Quebec. There he had gotten supplies long needed by the Mission: clothing, vessels for the altar, bread and wine for Mass, writing materials.

In his canoe and in those which followed was an even more precious cargo: thirty Christian Indians, most of them fresh from years of training under the Jesuits and the Ursuline nuns at Quebec. He was taking them to the Huron country. They would work among their own people as lay apostles. They would be an example of Christian living to the other Indians.

Père Isaac dug and pulled, his body moving in precisely the same rhythm as those of the four Indians paddling with him.

Happily his mind wandered back over the years. How difficult everything had been in the Huron country at first. How much better things had gone recently.

Out in the Huron country, three years before, the Jesuits had built a new Mission center. Sainte Marie, they had named it. It stood apart from any Huron village. Soon it would have its own fort, started under Isaac's direction the year before.

Père Isaac did some arithmetic in his head. Yes, in the last twelve months he and the other Jesuits at Sainte Marie had baptized at least a thousand Hurons. Some had been important chiefs, like Eustace. That was the Christian name of the steersman sitting ahead of Isaac in the canoe. He was a strong-featured man with glowing eyes. His Indian name was known in every village, for he was the bravest and most famous of all the Huron war chiefs.

Isaac let his paddle drift as Eustace, twisting his, headed the canoe toward a quiet inlet.

"We have gone far enough for one day, Père Isaac", said Eustace. "Little by little we come closer to our own villages. Tonight we camp here. We go on in the morning."

In the morning the little band of travelers held a conference on the river bank. A decision must be reached before they embarked on the second day of the long journey home. Eustace, the Huron war chief, led the discussion.

"My brothers," he said, "ahead of us are the islands. We can make our way through them by the southern route or the northern. Which shall it be?"

The Iroquois Indians, dreaded enemies of both the Hurons and the French, were on the warpath. Armed with muskets, sold to them illegally by Dutch traders, they had recently grown bolder and bolder. The southern route through the islands was open water. There were few forests along its banks where the Iroquois could wait in ambush. On the other hand, the northern route was a narrow channel between thickly-wooded shores.

"Danger", said Eustace, "awaits us along the northern route. But it is shorter and easier to paddle. I favor it."

In the end, after further debate, the others agreed. The canoes were floated. Soon they were in the northern channel, a threadlike path of water, sunless and still between the dark forests.

Suddenly Eustace halted the first canoe. He slipped overboard and waded shoreward. Père Isaac and several Indians followed. No one spoke. The Hurons gripped their tomahawks.

Reaching a clay bank close by the shore, Père Isaac looked at its gummy surface.

Footprints!

"Iroquois or Algonquin? Our enemies or our friends?" Père Isaac barely moved his lips.

The Indians were on their hands and knees, examining the footprints. They had trained themselves to "read" whatever they saw in the wilderness. The footprints told them much.

"Iroquois!" whispered Eustace. "But there cannot be more than three canoes of them. We are twelve canoes. Let us advance!"

They did so, cautiously, watchfully, their canoes strung out in single file. Shortly the stream widened. On their right, trees grew in the stagnant, scum-green waters of a swamp. Ahead, on their left, was a little cross-stream between islands. A danger point! Following Eustace's lead, the other steersmen edged their canoes toward the right, hugging the shallows along the line of trees.

And then it happened. *War whoops!*

They came, not from the cross-stream, but from the swamp on their right. Thirty Iroquois stood up among the waist-high weeds. Their muskets blazed.

Eustace drove the lead canoe toward them. Shouts and barking guns everywhere! Père Isaac felt a sharp, quivering crunch as the canoe struck a rock near the bank and turned over!

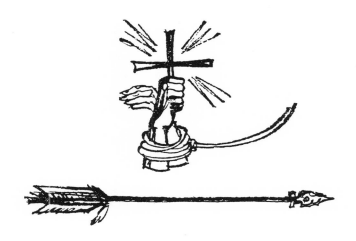

13

SLAVE OF THE MOHAWKS

Père Isaac swam under water as long as possible. When he surfaced, he found himself in a growth of thick weeds.

Cautiously, he parted some of the flat, broad leaves. Not a hundred feet from him, on the bank fringing the swamp, the Indians were battling. The enemies, he saw, were Mohawks, one of the fiercest of the five Iroquois nations.

A second and louder burst of war whoops reached him. Eight canoes shot out from the little cross-stream between the islands. Père Isaac's heart sank as the canoes beached and forty more Mohawks jumped out to join the battle.

It was all over now with the Hurons! Père Isaac saw half a dozen Mohawks pounce on Eustace. They bound his arms and legs with leather straps. A shout of triumph went up as the Mohawks saw that they had captured the greatest of the Huron war chiefs.

Isaac crouched as low as he could in the slimy water. Three Mohawks had waded into the swamp. He could hear them beating the nearby weeds with their spears, muttering to one another. He did not know their language but it was like that of the Hurons. He understood a phrase here and there.

He was wondering why there were so few of his own party on the bank, when a few words from one of the searching Mohawks told him all. At the first war whoop, half of the Hurons—all those in the rear canoes of the flotilla—had leaped into the water and escaped.

One of the Mohawks splashed by, so close that Isaac could have reached out and touched him. The other two followed, but not quite so near. He lifted himself a little. He could see the three searchers climbing the bank again, apparently satisfied that no one was hiding in the swamp.

Isaac realized that he was safe! He had only to wait until the Mohawks departed. He knew well now how to keep himself alive on the trail. He could easily make his way to the nearest French settlement.

Père Isaac shook his head. He scolded himself, thinking "What a weakling I am!" His friends were captives! They faced torture, possibly death. They needed their priest!

Pushing the weeds aside, Père Isaac saw that the Mohawks were loading their canoes, making ready to go. He got to his feet, showing himself. He signaled with his arm to attract the attention of the Mohawks and shouted to them.

For fourteen days the victorious Mohawks traveled, taking their captives with them. South they traveled, down the little Richelieu river and to the foot of Lake Champlain, then seventy miles over land.

Once they encountered a roving band of warriors from one of their own towns. The procession halted while the Mohawks showed off their captives.

"Behold!" they shouted. "Behold, we have seized the greatest of the Huron war chiefs, and many other Hurons besides. Behold, we have seized three of the hated Frenchmen, and one of them is a black-robe!"

A low platform was erected. On this, Père Isaac and his fellow captives were cruelly tortured.

It was a searing morning in late August when they at last looked down on the green and rolling valley of the Mohawks.

The conquerors were nearing home. They shouted their war songs. Braves ran along the line of captives, beating those who straggled, prodding the others with spears, sometimes forcing the captives to travel for miles at a dog-trot.

By noon they were far into the valley and were ascending a gradual incline above a river. At the crest of the hill was the strongly fortified village of Ossernenon, the Mohawk capital.

All the villagers had assembled on the plain along the river. From a distance, Isaac could see their activities. A platform had been erected. More torture! Already, the villagers were forming two long, parallel lines.

Père Isaac knew what that meant too. Once again, he and the other captives would have to run the gauntlet!

A shouting chief strode up and down between the lines.

"Welcome our captives!" he bellowed. "Caress them well!"

"*Welcome . . . caress!*" It was a devilish humor these Indians had. "Welcome . . . caress them!" meaning, "Torture them!"

As one of the most important of the prisoners, Père Isaac was the last man to be shoved between the lines of jeering Indians. In spite of his sufferings, he was still strong and fleet. He ran with all his might, wildly zig-zagging in an effort to duck the blows, kicks and stones that came at him from both sides. A hunk of iron, hurled by a shrieking squaw, caught him in the hip and knocked him, breathless, to the ground.

For a second, Père Isaac thought he could not go on. He knew he must. To lie here would mean death. At long last, his body a mass of cuts and blood, he reached the end of the line and staggered against the supporting poles of the platform.

There were several Mohawk villages. The prisoners were taken to all of them. In every town, it was the same story: the gauntlet! the torture platform!

In one of the villages, the chiefs held council. Next morning, Père Isaac was informed that he was to be burned at the stake. But during the day an argument broke out among the chiefs. Some favored letting the blackrobe live.

"Someday", these chiefs argued, "we Mohawks may tire of fighting the French. Someday we may find it to our advantage to trade with them as the Hurons do. The French love their blackrobes. If we kill this man, the French will never become our allies."

These arguments prevailed. At a second council, Isaac's sentence was revoked. A few days later, in the Mohawk capital of Ossernenon, he was taken to a cabin and handed over to an important chief as a slave.

The Mohawks had stripped Isaac of his cassock. For months, he had only a threadbare deerskin cape.

All fall he worked with the Mohawk women in the cornfields along the river. When winter came, the braves took him on a long hunting trip. They used him, as they did their squaws, for a pack horse.

Somehow, in spite of long days of hard work and cruel treatment, Père Isaac found time to study and master the Mohawk language.

Occasionally he was permitted to go to the other villages and visit with the people who had been captured with him. Eustace and some of the other Huron chieftains had been killed. Père Isaac instructed those who had survived and heard their confessions.

Spring came in a sudden burst of green. During the winter, Isaac had been lodged first with one family and then with another. He was living now in a cabin where the most important person was a vigorous old squaw.

In one way, the Mohawks—indeed all the Iroquois—were different from any other North American tribe. An intelligent woman could become a person of influence among them. This woman had. She sat at the council fire with the chiefs and ancients. Her opinions were respected. She liked Père Isaac. She called him "Nephew" and insisted that he regard her as "Aunt".

Returning from the fields one evening, Isaac found Aunt's cabin filled with bundled furs.

"Nephew," she said as he entered, "tomorrow, I go with a party of braves to trade with the Dutch. I have spoken with the chiefs. I have permission to take you with us."

Isaac could hardly believe his ears. For nine months, he had known almost no company but that of savages. That night, he could hardly sleep, realizing that tomorrow, once again, he would be among Europeans!

14

PÈRE ISAAC FINDS A FRIEND

FORTY MILES FROM THE MOHAWK CAPITAL, the low-slung cottages and barns of the Dutch settlement of Rensselaerswyck lay along the west bank of the Hudson river. It was nightfall when Isaac's Aunt and her party arrived and pitched camp on a clearing to the north.

Wherever Isaac went the next morning, two Indian guards accompanied him. They had strict orders from the old woman. Père Isaac was to go where he pleased. The Indians remained outside when, toward noon, he paid a call at the home of the Dutch minister.

A manservant opened the door. He looked at Père Isaac suspiciously, assuming, no doubt, that the worn-looking, poorly dressed man before him was some sort of beggar or tramp. Père Isaac gave him his name. "I am sure", he said, "that your master will know who I am."

"Wait here", said the servant coldly, closing the door and leaving Père Isaac standing on the street. A second later the door was reopened. This time the servant bowed his head courteously. "Come in, Père Isaac", he said. "My master is most anxious to see you." And he led Isaac to an open door on the far side of a gleaming kitchen.

Beyond was a small parlor, crowded with armchairs and an ornate sofa. The day was chilly. The flames of a pine fire leaped on a cobblestone hearth. As Isaac entered the room, a small, roly-poly man hurried to him with outstretched arms.

"Père Isaac!" he cried in a rolling, rumbly voice. "Is it really you? You are welcome in this house. Come, make yourself comfortable. And excuse me one minute. I have something for you. I have had it a long while."

Isaac sat down. He looked around at the neat, comfortable room; at the white covers on the armchairs; at the soft rug under his feet. He glanced at the mirror above the fireplace and sighed. It was hard to connect the haggard face reflected there with the robust young man who only seven years

before had stood on a ship in the Saint Lawrence
and gazed for the first time at the rock of Quebec!

A rat–ta–ta–tat of steps brought the Dutch minister into the room again. He placed a small black
book in Isaac's lap.

When Isaac looked at it, he gasped. It was his
breviary!

It had disappeared during the ambush, and he
had never dreamed he would see it again!

"But, Dominie . . . !" he began, his voice trem-
bling. The Dutch Calvinists called their minister
"Dominie". He tried to go on, but a sudden rush
of tears prevented.

"Good man!" cried the dominie. "That man is
a coward, I always say, who is afraid to weep when
weeping is called for!" He drew a chair close to
Isaac and settled himself. He was a pink-cheeked
little man with kind and laughing eyes. "Let me
explain how I came by this. Apparently one of
the savages picked it up when you were captured.
He brought it to the settlement here to sell it. I
saw what it was at once and bought it. How I
have longed to return it to you!"

"You could not have done me a greater kindness", said Père Isaac, who had gotten control of
himself again. "I thank you from the bottom of
my heart."

"Don't!" The dominie shot a tiny, fat hand
through the air. "I know what it means to you. I
do indeed, Père Isaac!" He squirmed forward, sit

ting on the edge of his chair. "When we heard here that the Mohawks had tortured and enslaved you, we were horrified. Our village director himself went out to the Mohawk village. Perhaps you saw him there."

Isaac nodded. "Yes, Dominie. I recall when your director visited the village."

"He asked the Mohawks to release you. He offered them money, a large sum of money. Many, many *gulden* indeed."

"That was very kind of your director."

"It was nothing!" Again the dominie's hand flew through the air, and he bounced in his chair. "Besides, it didn't work!" He made a face. He drew closer to Père Isaac and lowered his voice. "Père Isaac," he said, "the Indians will never free you of their own accord. We know. We have asked them countless times. We have offered them more *gulden*, and still more. Père Isaac, there is only one thing left to do. You must escape!"

"Escape!"

"With our help. We will arrange everything for you. Rest assured: with our help, you cannot fail. Yes, you will escape!"

"But, Dominie," Père Isaac said quietly, "other people were captured with me. Most of them are still among the Mohawks. Many are Christians. All are old friends. I am their priest. I could not leave them."

The Dutchman stared at Père Isaac. "But you

forget who you are!" he protested. "You are not only a priest. You are a gentleman of France. I hear these Indians treat you like a dog. I hear your life is in danger night and day, that anytime, any-where. . . ." The dominie broke off, as though horrified into silence by his own words.

Père Isaac dropped a hand on the other's knee.

"Do not think me ungrateful", he said. "I thank you for your kind offer. But, as I said before, I cannot leave my fellow captives."

Their eyes met. Those of the dominie were full of wonder.

15

PÈRE ISAAC WRITES A LETTER

THAT SUMMER THE IROQUOIS were again on the warpath. Père Isaac, back again in the Mohawk capital of Ossernenon, watched the war parties leave. For days the village lay silent in the sun, empty except for old men, women and children. With sinking heart, Père Isaac saw some of the war bands return. They brought with them the scalplocks of slain Hurons and Frenchmen.

The Mohawks bragged to Isaac. They described their victories and plans. They did this, he knew, to mock and distress him.

"We have fooled the French", a brave informed

123

him, as they stood one evening outside the cabin of Isaac's Aunt. "We have made them believe all our forces are along the Saint Lawrence. Behind their backs our warriors are slipping into the north, far above the Saint Lawrence. Soon we will cut off the trade route between the French settlements and the Huron country. Soon the French will no longer be able to trade with their Huron allies."

Turning to leave, the Indian threw a parting boast over his shoulder. "When that day comes," he gloated, "the French will have to go home."

The hot June night echoed with the song of insects. Père Isaac, hearing the soft pad of footsteps behind him, turned. It was a Mohawk war chief whom he had known for years. The chief was a Huron by birth. He had deserted his own people and joined the Mohawks. Among themselves, the Huron captives spoke of him as "the Renegade".

"I bring Ondessonk an offer", said the Renegade, addressing the Jesuit by his Huron name. "Will Ondessonk listen to a war chief's offer?"

"Ondessonk", said Isaac, "is listening."

"Good. Tomorrow, I lead my warriors to Fort Richelieu. Perhaps Ondessonk desires to write a letter to his French friends there. If so, let me have it. I will see that it is delivered."

Père Isaac saw through the Renegade's "offer". Fort Richelieu was new. The Mohawks had no idea how many cannon it had or how many French soldiers were inside. The Renegade hoped to use a letter from Père Isaac as a pretext. He would send a messenger with it, under a white flag, right up to the fort gate. The spy might even be invited inside where he could find out the information the Mohawks wanted.

Isaac's first thought was to say he did not care to write a letter. Then a better idea came to him.

"Come to my Aunt's cabin before you leave in the morning", he told the Renegade. "The letter will be ready for you."

The Dutch minister at Rensselaerswyck had given the Jesuit a supply of writing material. All night, crouching in the wavering light of the cabin fires, he composed his letter.

He described the Iroquois' plan to cut off the trade route between the French and the Hurons. He described the location of the Iroquois' summer war camps.

None of the Indians could read. But there was no telling into whose hands his letter might fall. So Père Isaac wrote it in three languages: French, Latin and Huron. He mixed the languages up so that only one of the Jesuits at the fort—a priest acquainted with all three languages as he himself was—could make sense of it.

Père Isaac addressed his letter to the commandant of Fort Richelieu. Dawn was filtering through the cabin cracks as he scratched the final words:

Be on your guard everywhere. There are seven hundred Iroquois warriors and they have three hundred arquebuses. They are skilled in handling them. I beg you that prayers be said and that Masses be offered for those of us who are captives here— and above all for the one who desires to be forever,

Monsieur,

Your very humble servant,

Isaac Jogues, of the Society of Jesus

From the village of the Iroquois,
the thirtieth of June, 1643.

16

DECISION

A FEW WEEKS LATER Isaac's Aunt and a band of
braves made another trading expedition to
the Dutch settlement of Rensselaerswyck. Père Isaac
was taken along.

When, once again, he stepped into the Dutch
minister's parlor, he was greeted even more warmly
than before. The dominie made Isaac comfortable
by the fire. He had his manservant prepare a meal
of wild fowl and rice. To Isaac, who for months
had tasted little but the unseasoned sagamite of
the Indians, it was a banquet.

Again, the dominie pleaded with Isaac to flee
his Mohawk masters.

"After all," he said, "the situation has changed since you were here last. I hear many of those who were captured with you have escaped."

It was true. During the summer, the Mohawks had taken some of their Huron captives on the warpath with them. From Mohawk camps, far to the north, these Hurons had slipped away. To the best of Isaac's knowledge, they were safe now among their own people.

"There is another thing", cried the minister. "The Mohawks are treacherous. I am surprised they have let you live this long. Any day, any hour, they may do away with you." The minister, as was his habit, bounced forward on his chair, his bright eyes snapping. "Tell me," he demanded, "when you are dead, what good will you be to your friends?"

Isaac smiled. "There is only one flaw in your argument, Dominie", he said. "I am not dead yet."

The minister chuckled.

He took Père Isaac to visit the important men of the settlement: the village director, the commandant of the fort, the leading burghers. They were good, kind men. They invited Père Isaac to dine at their homes. They took him to their taverns.

Père Isaac would not touch their cups of steaming wine for fear of setting a bad example to the Indians. Even so, the Dutch burghers found him good company. He laughed at their banter and traded them joke for joke. His quick wit drew many a roar from the Dutchmen as they lolled in their taverns, puffing their long-stemmed pipes.

They were stout and comfortable-looking men in their swelling knickerbockers and long black coats. In the worn deerskin cape that was still his only garment, Isaac cut a strange figure among them. Always lean and wiry, his sufferings had reduced him to a skeleton.

Like their minister, the burghers urged him to escape. He listened courteously, and shook his head. The Dutchmen shook theirs, amazed.

"Père Isaac," said one, "we are undecided whether to admire you as a hero or to scold you as a fool!"

One evening, as he walked across a clearing north of the settlement, Père Isaac saw a band of Mohawks approaching. They were shouting and bickering among themselves. He stood still, as one of them left the group and came running. With a piercing shout, the brave grabbed Isaac and hurled him to the ground. By now the others had arrived. They surrounded him. Listening to their excited cries, Père Isaac little by little figured out what had happened.

His letter—the letter he had written at the request of the chief back in the Mohawk capital! The Renegade and his war party had carried that letter to Fort Richelieu. As far as they knew, it was a harmless note from Père Isaac to his French friends there. Their plan was to send it to the French by messenger and so spy out the military strength of the new French fort.

But things did not turn out that way. The Indian messenger went up to the fort gate, carrying the letter and a flag of truce. The French let him in. Seeing this, the Renegade chief was delighted. "When our messenger returns," he told his warriors, "we will know how many cannon are in the fort and how many soldiers. Then we will know how to attack."

But the Mohawk messenger did not return. Père Isaac's letter was, of course, not just a friendly note. It was a detailed description of Iroquois battle plans. It was written in three languages, yes, but that did not bother the French officers. With the aid of the Jesuit priest stationed at the fort, they read it. Alarmed at its contents, they ordered their soldiers to fire on the Renegade and his party without delay.

The Mohawk warriors were taken by surprise. Many were killed. Two of their canoes were sunk. Crowding into the remaining canoes, the Mohawks fled in panic.

Arriving, after many days, in the Mohawk capital, they went at once to the cabin of Isaac's Aunt. Isaac's letter, they reasoned, had brought this disaster upon them. Their plan was to kill him on the spot. Learning that he was in Rensselaerswyck, they had followed him.

And now they encircled him, growling and threatening.

The brave who had thrown Isaac to the earth addressed him. "Two days only we stay in this place", he announced. "Then we return with the Indian traders. You will return with us. When we reach our own village, you will die!"

The warriors ordered Isaac to come with them. They were living in the barn of a Dutch farmer who had married a woman of their tribe.

That night, sleepless among the Indians, Père Isaac's mind was in turmoil. Again and again, the Mohawks had threatened him with death. He had learned to hope for the best, knowing that the Indians easily changed their minds. Often their anger was like a child's tantrum, afire one moment and gone the next.

This time, Père Isaac realized, the Mohawks were in earnest. Some of their finest warriors had been slain at Fort Richelieu. For this they blamed him.

He rose next morning with the Indians and breakfasted with them.

"Go where you wish in the settlement today", he was told. "But do not fail to return at night. Bear in mind that wherever you go, our eyes are on you!"

At midmorning, Isaac knocked at the door of

the Dutch minister's house. Word of his plight had already spread through the village. In the parlor, besides the minister, were the director and the commandant of the fort. They saw the look on Isaac's face as he entered, and met him with grim faces.

"Well, Père Isaac," said the dominie, "have you come to your senses?"

Père Isaac nodded. "I have thought long and hard", he told them. "I have prayed, for I want to do what is right. You know what lies ahead. There is no doubt about it—if I return to the Mohawk capital, the Indians will kill me. As you said the other day, Dominie—dead, I will be of no use to my friends."

He paused. By their expressions, the others showed that they sympathized with the struggle he had gone through to reach his decision.

"Gentlemen," said Père Isaac, "with your kind assistance, I shall try to escape!"

17

ESCAPE

THERE WERE TWO DOORS in the barn where the
Mohawk warriors and Père Isaac were sleeping. One of them led into the house of the Dutchman who owned the farm. The other led to a court
surrounded by a white picket fence.

Père Isaac, stretched out among the warriors,
mapped out the area in his mind. Everything was
ready for his escape. Out in the Hudson, anchored
at midstream, a Dutch sailing vessel waited to carry
him down the river.

A hundred yards from the ship, near the bank,
was a rowboat. Père Isaac knew the spot well. The

boat was tied to a tree stump just under a rocky incline at the far end of the open field that sloped from the farm to the river.

Père Isaac glanced at the cracks in the barn wall. It was still not quite dark. He would wait until he was certain all the Mohawks were asleep.

He closed his eyes, pretending to sleep. His senses, keyed up for what lay ahead, were painfully sharp. He could hear every rustle of the horses and cattle in the stalls at the end of the barn. He jumped at the screech of a nightbird, faint in the distance. The time passed with dreadful slowness.

At last, Isaac heard the Indians' regular breathing and knew that all were asleep. Then he lifted himself slowly to his feet.

He tugged at the heavy door into the court—and froze! He had gone in and out of this door several times. Never before had he noticed that the hinges were rusty and in need of oil.

There was only one thing to do: open it swiftly and hope that no Indian would hear the squeak.

Outside the night was cool and dark. There was no moon. Père Isaac was glad of that.

A few paces to his left was the door to the living section of the big farmhouse. Opposite it, in the picket fence, was a gate.

He ran lightly toward it and had almost reached it when a low and menacing growl came from the bushes along the fence.

Père Isaac stopped. Before he could determine what was happening, a huge dog was on him. He felt a sharp and sickening pain as, with another and louder growl, the beast sank its teeth into the calf of his leg.

Streaks of light shivered into the courtyard as the owner of the house hurried out, followed by his wife carrying a candelabra. A hoarse and mounting rumble of voices behind him told Père Isaac that the barn door had been thrown open. The Mohawk warriors crowded into the courtyard.

In the living room, the Dutch farmer applied salves to the Jesuit's bleeding leg. His wife, a Mohawk woman, wrapped it with damp towels.

The farmer was full of apologies. He had long known the dog was dangerous. He would chain it at once, and keep it chained.

Père Isaac had neither eyes nor ears for the Dutchman and his concern. He watched the Indians' faces, black with suspicion. He saw that they did not believe for one moment his tale of having stepped out for a breath of air. They sensed that he was trying to escape.

Back in the barn, he was not permitted to choose his own sleeping corner. Two husky braves placed him between them.

He found himself lying, as it were, in a human wedge. The deep gashes in his leg throbbed. He saw that if he moved to right or left, he would disturb one of his guards. To make matters worse, the Dutch farmer, at a muttered request from one of the Mohawks, went into the courtyard and barred the barn door from the outside.

Despair seized Père Isaac. He fought it off, telling himself he must not give up hope. At dawn, the warriors would depart for the Mohawk capital. He must flee tonight—or never!

The minutes dragged, slowly becoming hours. A faint light appeared along the cracks in the barn wall. The Indian on the right rolled over in his sleep, away from Isaac.

Now there was room. He could safely get to his feet. But what then? The courtyard door was barred. He considered slipping into the house itself, but abandoned the idea. He was bound to awaken either the farmer or his wife. Besides, the outer door of the house was most certainly locked.

His palms, soaking with sweat, clenched automatically as a shuffling sound reached his ears. Footsteps in the court! Someone was unbarring the door. It creaked open, and a flat, gray light filled the room.

It was one of the farmer's menservants, coming to feed the livestock. Père Isaac lifted himself cautiously. He signaled the man, making frantic gestures.

To his relief and surprise, the servant nodded. Putting down his feed buckets, he returned to the courtyard.

Père Isaac followed, stopping at the door to peer out.

The servant had understood him perfectly! He was standing alongside the big dog, patting the beast's head. He beckoned.

Père Isaac padded softly across the court and through the gate. In the open field, he ran harder than he had ever run before. A pink glow lay along the eastern horizon. Père Isaac ran harder, expecting at any moment to hear the angry shouts of the Mohawks behind him.

He reached the river bank and stumbled, or rather fell, to the beach below. For a second, he lay sprawled on the damp clay, gasping for breath. Then he searched the half-light for the rowboat.

A low moan escaped him. The Hudson was a tidal river. During the night, the waters had receded. The heavy boat, no longer afloat, was grounded.

He lunged at it, pushing. The strain of the night and the hard dash across the field had sapped his strength. The heavy boat did not budge. He ran to the front of it and pulled. Still the boat remained where it was, stuck in the sucking clay.

Père Isaac's mind raced. It was growing lighter. He was in full sight not only of the Dutch farm but of a row of hunting lodges set up by the trading Indians along the nearby hill.

He got behind the boat again. With a prayer on his lips, summoning his last ounce of strength, he gave another push. The boat quivered! Desperately, with his whole body, he pushed again. It moved again. And again. It nosed into the water, and floated!

Père Isaac jumped in, seizing the oars, and pushed off. A hundred yards down stream, gray and hulking in the dusty light, lay the Dutch sailing vessel— and possible freedom!

18

NEW AMSTERDAM

PÈRE ISAAC STEPPED LIGHTLY along the "Ditch"—
the main street of New Amsterdam, largest
of the Dutch settlements in the New World. He
wore the warm black cloak and beaver hat that
the Dutch had given him.

He had been brought down the Hudson by the
Dutch sailing vessel. In the gabled mansion within
the fort, the director-general of New Netherlands
had welcomed him with ceremony and great kindness. The director-general had lodged him first in
his own house. He was living now at the City
Tavern, a two-story stone building recently built

and regarded by the town's five hundred citizens with pride.

As he walked, Père Isaac noted with pleasure the neat Dutch houses, each with its garden plot. He was walking north. Not many yards behind him, at the foot of Manhattan Island, the great harbor sparkled under a clean autumn sky. At his left, on the Hudson, was the fort. Ahead, beginning where the village ended, were farmlands. In the distance Père Isaac could see the lazily turning arms of a windmill.

He turned and walked along Hoogh Street. He saw a roughly clad man coming his way and spoke to him. He did not know the man, but this was the custom among the friendly Dutch. Everyone greeted everyone else, friend or stranger.

The face that turned to Père Isaac was broad and pleasant and very young. The generous mouth spread in a happy grin, as the boy broke into a run. Dropping to his knees, he grabbed Père Isaac's hand.

"O Martyr!" he cried in a language that Père Isaac only vaguely understood. "O Martyr of Jesus Christ!"

New Amsterdam's citizens were a varied lot. Most were Dutch, yes, and members of the Calvinist Dutch Reformed church. But eighteen languages could be heard on the streets. Père Isaac had met people of many nationalities and religions, including his own. This boy's face, however, was new to him.

"Are you not a Calvinist?" he asked the lad.

"*Nenny!*" cried the boy. "Not at all!"

"Catholic then?"

"*Nenny! Polakim! Lutheranim!*"

A Polish Lutheran. Père Isaac lifted the smiling youth to his feet. He could not speak the boy's language, nor could the young Pole speak his. But their eyes spoke the admiration each felt for the other.

Some days later, a tall man dressed in the loose garments of a trader stepped into the Jesuit's room at City Tavern. The man spoke English, a language Père Isaac understood, and there was an easy roll in his voice that he had no trouble identifying.

He was an Irishman. Hearing that there was a priest among the Dutch, he had come all the way from Virginia to go to confession.

Père Isaac had heard of the English colony of Jamestown, founded in Virginia in 1607. Now, the Irishman told him, there were several settlements in Virginia with a combined population of 12,000 persons.

"And the English are sending over more settlers", said the Irishman. "And more and more. You French had better make haste, Father. Whoever owns this land will own a wonderful place. Sure, it's going to be a great country, with room in it for all, and food in it for all; yes, Father, and freedom for all!''

Père Isaac listened and marveled. He had learned so much in the last two years. He had stored it all in his memory until the day when he could rejoin his fellow Jesuits.

But when would that day come?

The Dutch had given him their solemn promise. He would be sent to France on the first ship that docked at New Amsterdam.

But the days passed, and no ship came.

The yellows and reds of autumn faded. The first snows dusted the cobblestones of the busy little seaport. Then one morning Père Isaac heard shouts outside the inn. He rushed into the street and followed the rejoicing villagers to the docks. The tubby ship bobbing over the horizon was the smallest sailing vessel he had ever seen. It was old and creaky and scarcely seaworthy.

"Never mind", said Père Isaac to himself. "It will carry me home!"

19

HOME AGAIN

EIGHT WEEKS LATER, Père Isaac was in the French city of Rennes. The Dutch vessel had brought him as far as England. A French coal boat had brought him the rest of the way.

Off the coast of England, while waiting to change ships, he had been set upon by thieves. He had lost the fine cloak the Dutch had given him in New Amsterdam and the fine beaver hat. The ragged garments he now wore were the gift of a French fisherman.

A winter dawn lighted the streets of Rennes as Père Isaac knocked at the door of the Jesuit college.

One hand clutched an official-looking paper. It was
a letter written by the director-general of New
Netherlands and stamped with his seal. It identified
Père Isaac. It related how he had escaped from the
Mohawks and how the Dutch had taken him under
their protection.

Père Isaac knocked again on the thick oak door.
He found it hard to believe that he was actually
home. To think that in a few minutes he would
once more clasp the hands of his fellow Jesuits!

In the drafty community room at the rear of
the college building, Brother Porter was laying a
fire on the big hearth. He heard the pounding on
the street door and frowned.

Brother Porter was feeling his years and his rheu-
matism this cold winter morning. He grumbled
under his breath as he limped down the long, damp
hallway. Decent people, he told himself, didn't
come visiting at this early hour.

He opened the street door and peered with dis-
taste at the bedraggled figure on the steps.

"I wish to see Father Rector", said Père Isaac.

"Sorry", said Brother Porter in a high, shaking
voice. "Father Rector is about to say Mass. If you
care to wait, you may do so here." He led Père
Isaac into a small parlor. "If you're in a great hurry,"
he added, "I'll call one of the other priests."

"I do not wish to see one of the other priests",

said Père Isaac firmly. "I wish to see Father Rector—
now!"

Brother Porter hobbled from the room, shaking
his head. "These beggars", he muttered to himself.
"Bold as kings, some of them!"

He pushed open the door to the sacristy and
called to Father Rector. "A poor man to see you.
I asked him to wait but he insists on seeing you
now."

Father Rector was vesting for Mass. "A poor
man?" he inquired.

"Poor in material things," squeaked Brother Porter, "but very rich in boldness."

Father Rector smiled. Brother Porter, he reflected, was never at his best on these cold winter
mornings. "A poor man", he repeated, half to himself and half to Brother Porter. "His need must
be great to bring him here so early."

He removed his vestments. He hurried down
the hall into the parlor.

It was very dark there behind the thick window
draperies. Father Rector took the letter that Père
Isaac thrust into his hand. He glanced at it in the
gleam of a single candle. His eyes picked up the
opening words only: "We, Willem Kieft, Director-
General, and the Council of the New Netherlands,
to all . . ."

He lay the letter on the table beside him. He

examined the face of his visitor, a worn and tired face under a rough peasant's cap.

"What is it we can do for you?" he asked gently.

"I come from Canada," said Père Isaac, "and I—"

He was not allowed to finish his sentence. "From Canada!" cried Father Rector. "From Canada, you say?"

"Yes, I have been there many years."

"Do you know any of our missioners there?"

"I know practically all of them."

"Good!" cried Father Rector. "Perhaps then you can tell me what everyone in France is longing to know. What of Père Isaac? Do the savage Iroquois still hold him? Is he alive?"

"He is alive. Indeed, he is free", Père Isaac's voice broke. He flung himself to his knees, grasping the older Jesuit's hands. "Father Rector," he cried, "it is he who speaks to you!"

Father Rector gasped. His eyes went from the letter on the table to the heavily lined face below him. With a cry that rang through the house, he pulled Père Isaac to his feet and embraced him.

He ran from the room. His voice echoed down the long corridor as he summoned the other priests.

They came quickly, filling the little parlor. They could not believe it at first; then they were amazed and delighted. They shouted. They laughed and cried at the same time as, one by one, they embraced

Père Isaac. Brother Porter was called. Open mouthed, he received the news. Then he hurried, squeaking, down the corridor—willingly this time—to procure a clean cassock for the welcome guest.

After Mass and breakfast, the Jesuits crowded into the community room. For hours they talked. Or rather, Père Isaac talked. The others listened, with wonderment and reverence.

Père Isaac did not remain long in Rennes. A few days later, in Orléans, he stepped from a stagecoach into his mother's arms.

In the living room where he had spent so much of his happy boyhood, the whole family had gathered: his sisters, all married now; his brothers, with their wives and children; his uncles, his cousins and his aunts.

Wine glasses were lifted. Eyes sparkled with laughter—yes, and with tears too. *Monsieur le Père* gave Isaac his own seat by the fire and hovered over his black-robed son, choking with pride and affection.

From Orléans, Isaac went by coach to Paris to visit his old school, the Jesuit College of Clermont. There too, he received a rousing welcome.

He was relieved when it was over, and he could sit down for a quiet talk with his Provincial Superior.

"Well, Isaac," said the older Jesuit, "do you wish to remain with us now, or to return to Canada?"

"To return", was the prompt reply.

"I thought you would say that. Very good. You will return to Canada as soon as a ship can be found to take you."

A few days later, a royal messenger appeared at the College of Clermont. Although the French court was in mourning, the messenger was dressed with vivid elegance: a long, lacy coat wrapped with a wide sash about the hips; baggy breeches trimmed with ribbon; a broad, heavily plumed hat over a wig of dangling corkscrew curls.

The messenger bowed deeply to Père Isaac, dusting the floor with his hat. He brought an invitation from Anne, the Queen Regent of France. Her majesty wished Père Isaac to visit her at the royal palace. Père Isaac muttered something about being very busy. He begged to be excused.

Only a few hours later, the messenger returned. This time he did not bring an invitation, but a command.

Père Isaac had no choice. At noon, the following day, he was ushered into the *Palais Royal*. The entire court had assembled: rows of powdered and perfumed women in wide-bustled dresses of brocade or satin; gentlemen in long coats of many colors and high-heeled slippers trimmed with stiff bows.

The queen sat on an armchair. She was dressed simply, for her husband, Louis XIII, had died only the previous May. Beside her stood a five-year-old boy. A bright-eyed lad, he held his head proudly above a white shirt, trimmed with a broad, flat collar. He was the King of France, Louis XIV.

The queen asked Isaac many questions. He spoke little of his torture and captivity. He did repeat to Queen Anne what the Irishman from Virginia had told him in New Amsterdam: that in the New World there was room and food and freedom for everyone.

20

THE TOMAHAWK FALLS

O N THE AFTERNOON of September 25, 1646,
Père Isaac, a young Frenchman named La
Lande, and a small band of Indians made camp
on a hill overlooking the meeting point of the Saint
Lawrence and Richelieu Rivers.

Père Isaac had been back in Canada for over a
year. Great events had taken place. At long last,
the warring Mohawks had agreed to hold council
with the French. Other councils had followed, and
finally a treaty. For the first time in almost forty
years, peace reigned between the French and their
Iroquois enemies.

While his companions prepared the evening meal, Père Isaac walked up the hill toward what remained of Fort Richelieu. The French had abandoned it two years before. Already the crumbling walls were covered with heavy vines.

As Père Isaac reached the hilltop, a buzzard flew from the underbrush. With a sound like the tearing of paper, the frightened bird lifted itself heavily. Isaac watched it winging west, gradually becoming just a moving blot in a cloudless sky. He walked on, through what had been the fort gate. In the courtyard, he kicked his way among the ruins of former barracks and the damp, green growth of two summers.

He heard his name called. Turning, he saw La Lande, the young Frenchman, at the crown of the hill.

"What is it, my boy?"

"Come quickly, *mon Père!*" The young man was breathless. "Some are leaving us."

"Some? Who?"

"All of the Iroquois and some of the Hurons too!"

Père Isaac hurried past the boy and down the hill. Halfway down, he stopped, his eyes on the Saint Lawrence below. It was too late, he saw, to stop the Iroquois. He could see their frail canoe streaking eastward on the river, leaving behind a line of silver ripples.

Père Isaac hurried on. The Hurons had gathered on the river bank. He could hear their voices, loud and angry. As he arrived, they became silent. His eyes went to a stocky, broad-faced chieftain.

"Well?"

"Do not ask me, Ondessonk", said the chief, using the Jesuit's Huron name. "Ask them!" He pointed to the young braves, huddled together near the water's edge. "They are the ones who wish to leave us."

"Why?" Père Isaac turned to the others. His eyes traveled from face to face. "Why?" he repeated. "You came with us willingly when we left Three Rivers this morning. We still have many leagues to go. Why have you changed your minds?"

The huddled Hurons glanced at each other, avoiding Père Isaac's level gaze. "Tell me, one of you!" he demanded. "Why do you choose to leave us?"

A slender brave stepped forward. He met Isaac's eyes uncertainly. "Ondessonk, I will tell you. I do not like to admit it, but we are afraid."

"Afraid of what?"

"Of the Mohawks."

"But why?"

"You know why. Tell me, Ondessonk, how many months did you live in the Mohawk capital as a slave?"

"Many months", Père Isaac jabbed the air with

his hand impatiently. "What has that to do with this?"

"Did you not find the Mohawks cruel and treacherous?"

"The Mohawks were our enemies then and I was a slave. They are friends now. I go to them this time, not as a slave, but as a missionary. It is different."

"How do you know it will be different?"

"I know what you know. You sat at the council fires in Quebec and Three Rivers. You saw the peace treaty arranged. You heard what was said there."

"Yes", the slender brave nodded. "I heard what was said there. But I have heard other things since."

"What other things?"

"I have heard that the Mohawks are quarreling among themselves. Some say the peace treaty helps the French, but does not help the Iroquois. Some favor digging up the war hatchet!" The young brave drew closer to Isaac, his voice suddenly pleading, almost tender. "Ondessonk, if you value your life, return with us to Three Rivers. Do not make this journey."

"I asked the Mohawks to accept me as a missionary", said Père Isaac. "They agreed to do so. I will live among them this winter, as I once lived among your people, teaching them and tending the sick." Again Isaac's eyes went from face to

face. Some of the Huron braves hung their heads.
"I must go on this journey", said the Jesuit quietly.
"And now—how many of you are going with me?"

No one answered. In silence the Hurons trooped
down the bank and climbed into their canoes.

Père Isaac watched them push off. Earlier in the
afternoon, there had been three canoes on the river
bank. There was only one now.

Père Isaac looked from side to side, woefully.
Of the little band that had embarked with him at
dawn, only two remained: the broad-faced Huron
chief and La Lande, the young Jesuit lay brother.

For many days the little group traveled south. Once
before Père Isaac had made this journey. It was
the very route he had taken as a captive of the
Mohawks. Sad memories crowded his mind as the
canoe slid past the island in Lake Champlain where
four years before he had stood on a Mohawk torture
platform for the first time.

And now he was going to the villages of those
who had tortured him as he had long wished to
go—as a teacher and a friend.

As they paddled steadily down the long lake,
cold weather came to meet them. One day the
forests at their right were gaudy with the burning
colors of autumn. The very next morning, they
were gray. A wintery wind mourned in the spruce
trees.

They reached the end of the water route and began the seventy-mile journey over land to the valley of the Mohawks. The trail was slick with half-frozen leaves. Descending a steep bank above a bustling stream, they dug their heels into the crumbly, half-frozen earth.

Suddenly, as though a door had opened in the forest, a band of Mohawk warriors appeared. Père Isaac lifted his hand and shouted a greeting. His words still hung in the air when, as suddenly as they had appeared, the Indians vanished. It was as though the trunks of the towering trees had opened and received them.

The travelers exchanged glances.

The eyes of the broad-faced Huron chief narrowed to a worried slit. Those of La Lande, the young Frenchman, popped open. Born and brought up in France, La Lande, on coming to the New World, had joined the Jesuits as a lay brother. He was a woodsman by training, but he knew little of Indians.

His eyes questioned Père Isaac. "Only a second ago they were right here. Now they are gone. How can this be?"

"An Indian", said Isaac, "can stand a few feet from you in the forest and make himself invisible." He turned to the Huron chieftain. "I do not understand", he said. "Why did they not return my greeting?"

The chief's narrowed eyes roamed the dense forest around them. "I do not like this", he murmured, more to himself than to Isaac. "There is something here that is not right. Call them again, Ondessonk."

Père Isaac did so. His words ran along the forest corridors. The echoes returned faintly, from afar, and faded.

They stood in a pool of frozen silence.

But not for long. In a deafening burst of sound, the Mohawks reappeared. This time they came from all sides, shrieking, howling, waving their muskets and tomahawks. They formed a moving circle around them, stamping the earth in a wild war dance.

Père Isaac stared at them, baffled. "But we are at peace", he told himself, only half believing his own words. "These Indians can mean us no harm. They must be making believe. Yes, making believe!" He waved at the dancing warriors. He made faces. He pretended to laugh at them.

No laughter came from the Indians. Terrified, he saw the crimson-painted warriors break ranks. They swept toward him. He felt himself being hurled to the ground. Rude hands stripped the cassock from his body. A stone gashed his forehead. He closed his eyes against a blinding rush of blood.

The din around him increased. Unable to see or hear anything clearly, he was vaguely aware that more Indians had appeared, rushing out of the forest.

He was being lifted and pushed forward. The hands that held him were rough, but he sensed that they were friendly.

He opened his eyes, taking in the scene before him through a veil of blood. He was being hurried up a hill, toward a wall-like structure. Suddenly, he realized where he was. He knew this scene. It was all there, stored forever in his memory. This was Ossernenon, the Mohawk capital.

He was rushed through the palisade gate, through the streets, into a cabin full of bitter smoke and shouting Indians. He became aware of a face close to his own, the face of an old woman, a face he knew and loved! It was the squaw who had first taken him to visit the Dutch. It was his Mohawk Aunt! The old woman's arms opened. She folded Père Isaac to her breast.

He could hear her words, harsh but soft under the surrounding noise. "Be calm, my nephew, be calm. You are home. You are safe. You and your friends—all are safe!"

Père Isaac slept and half-awakened. He slept again and awakened.

Slowly the scene around him arranged itself. It was the cabin he knew so well, the cabin of his Mohawk Aunt. La Lande's fresh young face grinned at him from across the room. The broad-faced Huron chieftain and Isaac's Aunt sat nearby, close to the fire.

"So you are awake, Ondessonk", said the woman softly.

Père Isaac looked around questioningly. Golden sun filled the cracks of the cabin.

"It is day again?" he inquired.

"Yes, Ondessonk. You have slept all night." The old woman came toward him, moving with her usual dignity. She placed a bowl of steaming sagamite flavored with fish in his hand. "Eat, my Nephew. Then I shall explain everything."

Père Isaac ate hungrily. He was glad of the warmth of the food, of the quiet of the smoky cabin.

The old woman sat beside him, talking in a low voice. "Dark days have come upon us", she said. "Perhaps you have heard."

"I hear that some of the Mohawks do not like the peace."

The old woman sighed. "Some of our braves", she said, "continue to hate the French. They are the ones who attacked you yesterday. Fortunately, other braves—men who would keep the peace— were here in the village. They heard the shouts in the forest. It was they who rescued you."

"My Aunt," said Père Isaac. "I come this time as a missionary. Will I be permitted to remain and work here?"

The old woman rose. "I go now to a council with the chiefs", she said. "When I return, I will know the answer to your question." She pointed to a row of barrels on the platform along the cabin wall. "There is plenty of food here and plenty of firewood. Under pain of death, do not leave the cabin until I return."

She nodded to the others and went out.

Père Isaac and his two companions talked. Occasionally, and for short spells, they slept. Toward evening, as the autumn dusk closed in, they prepared their supper.

Hearing footsteps outside the cabin, Père Isaac hurried to the door. He was eager to hear what had been decided at the council fire. But it was not his Aunt. A young brave stood on the porch.

The Mohawk lifted his arm. "Welcome again to the Mohawk villages, Ondessonk", he said, and Père Isaac did not like the sound of his voice. "I bring you an invitation. There is a feast at my house. You will follow me."

"One minute", Père Isaac went to a corner of the cabin. From among some belongings he lifted a small Rosary.

As he turned to leave, young La Lande leaped to his feet. The French youth placed himself at the door, barring the way.

"*Mon Père*," he begged, "do not go! The old woman said we must remain here till she returns. How do you know this is not some trick?"

"It may be", said Isaac quietly. "All the same, I will go."

"But, *mon Père!*"

"As a missionary", said the Jesuit, "I must respect the Indians' customs. To refuse an invitation to a feast is to make an enemy for life."

He dropped his hand on the youth's shoulder. Gently pushing the lad aside, he lifted the door flap and went out.

The Indian was still on the porch. They walked together, in silence, through the dark streets, stopping before a large longhouse decorated with the roughly carved figure of a bear. It was not a cold night, only brisk. Clean-cut stars glistened in the darkening sky. The tangy fragrance of frostbitten apples hung in the air.

The Mohawk pulled aside the deerskin covering the door. "Enter, Ondessonk", he said, indicating that Père Isaac was to go first.

The door was low. The Jesuit was not a tall man. Even so, he was forced to bow his head.

Inside, in the shadows, a Mohawk brave waited— a tall, handsome man with a slanting black scar along his left cheek.

As Père Isaac entered, the tall Mohawk lowered his tomahawk. Père Isaac knew only a single, fleeting flash of pain before becoming God's own.

It was about six o'clock in the evening. The date was October 18, 1646.

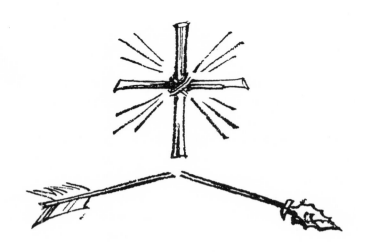

21

INDIAN AND SAINT

ONDESSONK WAS DEAD.
The news drifted through the Indian villages like a sad breeze.

There was mourning in the Huron cabins, and in Iroquois cabins too, for many Mohawks had come to love and admire the brave blackrobe.

Père Isaac's Aunt gathered together his few belongings and carried them to Rensselaerswyck. When she handed them to the Dutch minister, the dominie wept.

No one, anywhere, was more grieved than a sturdy young Frenchman named Jean Amyot—the same Jean, who, as a solemn, freckle-faced lad of ten, had gone with Père Isaac to the Huron country ten years before.

Jean had grown to manhood among the Indians, first in the Huron cabins and later among the Algonquins near Quebec. In the fall of 1647, he led a band of Algonquins on a scouting expedition. The Iroquois had dug up the war hatchet. They had broken the peace. All summer, along the Saint Lawrence, they had attacked and robbed.

In a forest clearing, not far from Quebec, Jean Amyot and the Algonquins met and defeated an Iroquois war party. Seven Iroquois were slain. As the victors were about to depart, Jean Amyot discovered an enemy brave hiding in the hollow trunk of a tree.

The captive was a Mohawk—a tall, handsome man. The Algonquins promptly nicknamed him the "Scarred One" because of the slanting black scar along his left cheek.

They took him to Quebec. Living there were several Hurons who had been in the Mohawk capital, as captives, at the time of Père Isaac's death. When these Hurons saw the Scarred One, they muttered among themselves.

Soon a strange rumor was heard on all sides. The Scarred One, people said, is Père Isaac's murderer!

Word of the rumor reached the French governor. He called the tall Mohawk and questioned him. "Were you in the Mohawk capital on the night of Père Isaac's death?" he asked.

"Yes", said the Indian. "I was there."

"Was Père Isaac's death ordered by your chieftains?"

"No. It was not."

"Why then was he killed?"

"Because some Mohawk braves were determined to destroy all Frenchmen."

The governor conferred with his aides. He turned back to the scarred Mohawk. "Some Hurons", he said, "say that you yourself killed Père Isaac. Did you?"

The Indian did not answer. He had answered all the other questions forthrightly. Now he was silent.

The French governor repeated the question. This time, the tall Mohawk merely hung his head.

The governor conferred again with his aides. "We cannot execute this man", he said. "The Hurons say he is guilty. I myself believe he is. But no one here actually saw the murder committed. We must let this man go."

Leaving the fort, the Mohawk brave went at once to the Jesuit Mission house in Quebec. Several of the priests were present.

"I am here", he told them, "to request of you the waters-of-importance." He spoke in the Indian manner. "Waters-of-importance" was their phrase for the waters of baptism.

The Jesuits looked at one another, amazed. They too believed that this was the Indian who had killed Père Isaac.

He noted their expressions. "I speak in earnest", he assured them. "I wish to go to heaven. I am sorry to have offended Him-Who-Made-All. We must all appear before him, according to your saying. At that time you may say I have been false if my heart has not now the belief which my mouth declares to you."

His words moved the Jesuits. They instructed him. They found that he knew the beliefs of their Faith and was wholly sincere. On September 16, 1647, the tall Mohawk was baptized and given the Christian name of Isaac Jogues. Soon after, the Algonquins took him away to one of their villages. There, sometime the following month, they executed him.

News of this reached Quebec in the late winter. There were several versions of what had happened. Some said the Scarred One had admitted his guilt just before he died. Others said that he had remained silent to the end. On one thing all agreed. The Indian Isaac Jogues had died, as the Jesuit Isaac

Jogues had died before him, in the Faith and like a man.

The name did not die with him. On June 29, 1930, Pope Pius XI raised Père Isaac Jogues to the Altars of the Church. Today, he who was known to all the Indians of his time and place as Ondessonk, is known to all the world as Saint Isaac.

ACCORDING TO HISTORY

THIS STORY OF SAINT ISAAC is based on historical
facts.

The author relied, principally, on four books:

1. The *Jesuit Relations*. These documents are eye-witness accounts written by the seventeenth-century Jesuit missionaries. The complete English translation is edited by Reuben Gold Thwaites and published in 73 volumes (Burrows, 1896–1901).

2. *Saint among Savages: The Life of Isaac Jogues*, by the Rev. Francis X. Talbot, S. J. (Harper, 1935).

3. *Saint among the Hurons: The Life of Jean de Brébeuf*, also by Father Talbot (Harper, 1949).

4. *The Jesuits in North America in the Seventeenth Century*, by Francis Parkman (Little Brown, 1867).

The Christmas carol on page 75, which was taught to the Indians by Père Jean de Brébeuf, was still being sung by the Hurons more than one hundred years later. Father DeVilleneuve, a Jesuit, was stationed at Lorette, Canada, between 1747 and 1749. It was in Lorette that the few remaining members of the Huron nation had lived since 1650. There Father DeVilleneuve heard the Indians sing the carol. They told him that Saint Jean had written it and taught it to their ancestors. The carol was first printed, in French, in Ernest Myrand's book *Old Carols of New France*. The version used here appeared in 1927 in *The First Canadian Christmas Carol*, published by Rous and Mann, Ltd., of Toronto. J. R. Middleton has translated the carol; it is not a strict translation from either the Huron or the French languages.

Today, famous monuments stand at two of the places where Saint Isaac lived and worked. The Shrine of the American Martyrs, near Midland, Ontario, Canada, overlooks the ruins of the fort of Sainte Marie Mission—the fort that was begun under Saint Isaac's direction. The ruins are on the east bank of the Wye river, ninety miles above Toronto. The Shrine of the North American Martyrs is in Auriesville, town of Glen, Montgomery County, New York. It marks the site of the Mohawk village where Saint Isaac lived as a slave and where he was killed.

Quebec and Three Rivers are now large Canadian cities. The Quebec post office stands on the site of the fort whose cannon welcomed Saint Isaac to the New World. A statue of the Sacred Heart, at the corner of the Rue du Chateau and Notre Dame, marks the site of the mission house where he spent his first night in Quebec.

Tiny Township of Simcoe County, Ontario, embraces the area where Ihonatiria ("The-Little-Hamlet-above-the-Loaded-Canoes") stood in Saint Isaac's day.

Authorities are not quite certain where Saint Isaac was ambushed and captured by the Mohawks. It happened somewhere along the North Channel of the Saint Lawrence River, probably opposite the Ile à l'Aigle near the boundary between Berthier and Maskinonge counties in the Canadian province of Quebec.

Today, if you wish to tread where Saint Isaac did in Rensselaerswyck, you have only to walk along Broadway, James Street, Court Street, State Street and Pearl Street in Albany, New York.

And New York City, of course, has grown out of New Amsterdam. Saint Isaac was the first Catholic priest to set foot in what was to become the world's largest metropolis. In his day, to be sure, New York was only a tiny village at the bottom of Manhattan island. Hoogh Street, where Saint Isaac met the Polish Lutheran lad, is now High Street. The "Ditch" is now Broad Street. On the steps of the old building at the north end of this thoroughfare—a building that still stands—George Washington took the oath of office as the first president of the United States.

A few words, finally, about some of the other people mentioned in the story or closely connected with the events it covers:

As a young man, Jean Amyot realized his boyhood ambition to become an interpreter. For several years he served the Jesuits of New France in that position. On May 23, 1648—only two years after Saint Isaac's martyrdom—while crossing the Saint Lawrence near Three Rivers, Jean's canoe was upset by a sudden storm and he and a fellow interpreter were drowned. After his death, a Jesuit who had known Jean praised him for his "skill and courage" and wrote that "in the opinion of all the country, his was a blameless life." Many others remarked on the faithfulness with which Jean, throughout his brief life, held to the teachings of the saintly companion of his boyhood.

Saint Isaac was one of eight seventeenth-century Jesuit missionaries to be martyred by the Indians.

Saint Jean de Brébeuf, Isaac's first superior in the Huron country, was burned at the stake by the Iroquois in 1649.

Saint Jean de La Lande was killed by the Mohawks on the same night (October 18, 1646) that Saint Isaac was killed.

Saint René Goupil, a Jesuit lay brother captured with Saint Isaac in the Mohawk ambush, was tomahawked by two Iroquois braves in the fall of 1642.

All the others were killed by the Iroquois in 1649. They are Saints Antoine Daniel, Charles Garnier, Noel Chabanel and Gabriel Lalemant.

The feast day for all the Jesuit Martyrs of North America is October 19.

For some notion of what Saint Isaac looked like, see the picture of him in the front of Father Talbot's biography *Saint Among Savages*. There is a statue of him on the brass doors of Saint Patrick's Cathedral in New York City. This lovely figure, sculptured by John Angel, shows Saint Isaac in his cassock. His left hand is raised. In it, of course, is the cross.